MASKS

A
MELANIE KROUPA
BOOK

MASKS

by Gloria Hatrick

Orchard Books

New York

Orchard Books
95 Madison Avenue
New York, NY 10016

Manufactured in the United States of America
Book design by Chris Hammill Paul

10 9 8 7 6 5 4 3 2 1

The text of this book is set in 11 point Palatino.

Library of Congress Cataloging-in-Publication Data
Hatrick, Gloria.
     Masks / by Gloria Hatrick. — 1st American ed.
        p.   cm.
     "A Melanie Kroupa book"—Half t.p.
     "First published in Great Britain by Julia MacRae Books in 1992"—
T.p. verso.
     Summary: Desperate to help his older brother Will who has become
paralyzed by a rare disease, Pete uses tribal animal masks to communicate
with Will, allowing him to escape his useless body and embark on a series
of strange and powerful dream journeys.
     ISBN 0-531-09514-2. —ISBN 0-531-08864-2 (lib. bdg.)
     [1. Guillain-Barré syndrome—Fiction. 2. Brothers—Fiction.
3. Physically handicapped—Fiction. 4. Dreams—Fiction.]
I. Title.
PZ7.H2845Mas   1996
[Fic]—dc20   95-38070

This one's for you, Mom

Our hands were firmly cemented
With a fast balm, which thence did spring.
Our eye-beams twisted and did thread
Our eyes upon one double string.

—John Donne

CHAPTER ONE

"HE'S EASY. Polyester pajamas with a paisley print, thigh-length navy-blue bathrobe, worn thin on the butt."

"Bull's-eye. Slippers?"

"Brown imitation leather."

"Um. Gets a new pair every Christmas from the wife."

"You got it, Pete. Your turn. I'll find a victim." Will scanned the airport crowd while we waited for our bags to be regurgitated through the hole in the center of the conveyor belt. The pajama game was one of our favorite time killers when we got bored. All you had to do was imagine what people slept in or wore first thing in the morning. Pajamas could tell you lots about people. Will was terrific at it.

"Got one," he said.

I looked. This incredibly built guy was standing in line. He had muscles in his earlobes. You could see he was flexing just for fun while he stood there.

I concentrated. "Snoopy nightshirt?"

Will laughed and shook his head.

"I give up. What's he sleep in?"

"Pajamas with feet." Will had grabbed my head and stuck it under his arm like a football.

"Will. The bags are coming up." Dad's voice ended our game. He and Mom had been in the snack bar, trying to relax after our long flight home from England. We were coming back from five weeks of castles, pub grub, and relatives from Yorkshire on Dad's side.

"Okay." Will let go, and we made our way to the conveyor belt.

People were jostling one another, trying to get their stuff first. Will started talking to some guy in a wheelchair. The next thing I knew, he'd grabbed the guy's small backpack off the belt.

"Want some help through customs?" he asked.

The man thanked him and said he could manage. Will wheeled him free of the crowd.

I think about that now and wonder if it was some kind of warning, an omen. Even if it was, I couldn't have done anything to stop what was coming. But I would have tried.

"Can you see our stuff yet?" Will asked.

"Yeah. Here it comes. It's all there."

I think that was when I first noticed something was wrong. The belt slowly bumped our bags around to us. Will reached out for the big suitcase that had most of Mom and Dad's stuff in it. He had a hold of it, but as the conveyor belt moved it around, he just kind of let go. It went on by as I grabbed the two backpacks.

"Good going, Will," I joked as we waited for it to come around again.

"Just practicing," he joked back.

I slipped into my backpack. Will got one strap over his shoulder but couldn't get his arm through the other one. I had to help him. That was the second odd thing. Then the big suitcase eventually came around, and he reached for it again. The same thing happened. He made a grab for it and then just let go. I saved it.

"What's Mom got in there?" he asked. "Half the Pennine Mountains?"

It was strange, because the bag didn't seem especially heavy to me. And I'm kind of a wimp compared to Will.

Anyway, we got through customs and home. We were all dead tired.

"Straight to bed, you two," Mom said. "We can unpack tomorrow."

I was all for that and took the stairs two at a time. Will started up after me but only made it halfway before he sat down. We should have known then, but I just figured it was jet lag. If only it had been that simple.

"What's up, Will? Too much jet-setting?" Dad said.

Will smiled and shook his head. I hoisted him up piggyback, stumbling most of the way with him singing, loud and off-key in my left ear, *"He Ain't Heavy ... He's My Brother."*

The real problems began the next morning. Will slept late. Finally, after the rest of us had eaten breakfast and looked at the mail, and Dad had complained about the vacation bills that were already starting to come in, I went upstairs to wrestle him out of bed. But he was just lying there, awake.

"Hey, Pedro, can you get my Walkman for me? I'm too tired to get up."

"Lazybones." I laughed, sitting on his stomach. "Get

3

up, you big jock. What's the matter, you turning into a couch potato?" I was bouncing up and down on him, and he was laughing. I was waiting for him to get fed up and send me flying or pin me down, but he didn't.

"You okay?" I asked.

"Course I am. Just tired. Hand me my Walkman, will you?"

I tossed it to him, but he didn't even try to catch it. Instead, he pulled himself up slowly in bed, like an old man. Then he fiddled around with the headset, trying to untangle it. He was all thumbs.

"It would help if you opened your eyes," I suggested. His eyelids were at half-mast, like he was drunk.

"Damn." He finally gave up and slumped back in his bed. "Just let me sleep awhile longer, Pete. I'm really dead tired." He turned toward the wall, and even that seemed to be an effort.

I started unpacking, trying to find room for all the cool junk we'd gotten in England. Mom always says we're born pack rats, just like Dad.

"Hey, Will, you're going to have to give up sports. With all these trophies, there's no room on the shelves."

"Throw them in the closet, Pete. They just collect dust anyway."

I was looking at the stuff we'd brought back from the vacation—a cricket bat, a rugby ball, some hedgehog quills, Roman coins, and loads of empty potato-chip bags. They have potato chips, or crisps as they call them in England, in every flavor you can think of, even roast beef. We'd lived on them all summer.

I kept noticing Will moving around in his bed. Finally, he turned toward me. "Damn covers are all twisted up.

My feet keep falling asleep—you know, pins and needles. Maybe I'd better get up and walk around." He pushed the blanket away and grabbed his legs at the knees. He tugged them up and over the edge of the bed. "Man, I feel peculiar. Give me a hand, will you, Pete?"

I did my usual thing when someone asks for a hand. I clapped.

"Very funny. Now cut the clowning and help me up."

I walked to the side of his bed and grabbed his extended hands, waiting for him to pull me down onto the bed, but he didn't. He just sat there. "Pull," he said.

So I pulled. "Jeez, Will, you've definitely had too much fish and chips. Or maybe it was all those potato chips. I warned you not to eat those Worcestershire-sauce ones." I was tugging away the whole time.

"Stop talking a minute and just concentrate," Will said. He sounded angry.

I still thought he was kidding, teasing me. So I grabbed him under the arms and bent my legs, keeping my back straight.

"Cheeeeeeeeow," I shouted. This was my imitation of a Japanese sumo wrestler. Will and I love sumo.

"What's going on here?" It was Mom. She came into the room just as I had Will on his feet.

"Nothing. I'm just trying to get this big lug out of bed. Too much Old World fun, Mom."

She laughed and turned to leave. "Get yourselves unpacked. It gets worse if you leave it."

Will and I stood, me with my hands under his arms. "Wanna dance, big boy?" I said, winking at his half-shut stare.

"Christ, my legs really are asleep, Pete. I don't think I can walk."

5

The game was getting old, but if there's one thing Will is, it's stubborn. I'd play along for a while, waiting for him to make his attack.

"For crying out loud, boys, stop messing around. We have too much to do today." I turned my head to see Dad. He stood in the doorway, looking at me holding Will.

Will took the opportunity to lunge forward, catching me off-balance. All hell broke loose as we both went over, crashing to the floor and taking half the shelves with us.

Dad was shouting, Mom was asking what on earth was going on, and I couldn't stop laughing. Only Will was quiet.

He was on top of me, a dead weight. My arms and legs were pinned. His head rested heavily on my shoulder.

I turned to look at him, and what I saw made me stop laughing. His half-shut eyes looked confused, like he couldn't focus.

"You okay, buddy?" I whispered.

"I don't think so, Pedro."

The next few hours are a blur. We got Will to the doctor, and he didn't know what was wrong, so he sent us to the hospital. Different people kept seeing him in the emergency room. They X-rayed his head and hips. It all happened so quickly.

The only thing I can remember really clearly is when they stuck us in a waiting room while they did some test. Me and Mom and Dad. I don't think we were in there long, but it seemed like forever. I couldn't sit still. I was walking back and forth, like an animal in a cage. Mom and Dad were sitting there, holding each other's hands.

I felt like I was going to explode, like I wanted to put

my fist through the little round window in the waiting-room door.

And then the specialist came in. His name was Dr. Woodson.

"Where's Will?" I almost shouted the question, but I just wanted to see him, to see that he was okay.

Dr. Woodson was wearing these little Ben Franklin kind of glasses. He peered over them at Mom and Dad. He didn't look at me.

"Your son's being taken up to pediatrics. We're going to have to keep him for a while."

I didn't wait to hear the rest. Mom and Dad could fill me in later. I just wanted to see Will, so I headed straight for a sign that said PEDIATRICS.

When I got there, I was feeling nervous. The place was creepy. There were lots of kids, most of them much younger than Will. But they were really quiet. Too quiet. And the place smelled bad, too, like a bottle of vitamins when you first open it.

I heard this strange sound in the hall. Kind of a *clunk, clunk, tinkle, tinkle.* It was a cart loaded with bottles with someone all white and starched pushing it. She looked like she was in charge, so I followed her. She was moving fast. I nearly had to jog to catch up with her.

"Excuse me," I said when she finally stopped. "I'm looking for my brother, Will Chisholm."

She looked at a little upside-down watch that hung on her uniform. A badge right above it told me she was A. Kirby, RN, whatever that was.

"Yes," she said. "The new patient. I'm on my way to him now. Follow me."

We clanked and tinkled down to the end of the hall, where she turned in to a room with four beds. Two of them were empty.

Will was in a wheelchair, kind of napping, while a couple of nurses were busy getting his bed ready.

"Can I take him onto the patio?" I asked, noticing sliding glass doors. I was dying to get him out of the place, to breathe some fresh air.

Ms. Kirby looked doubtful. "It's not a very nice day."

"I could really use some fresh air," I said. "And Will loves to be outside."

She nodded and helped me get the chair over the frame of the glass doors and onto the patio.

"Don't leave this spot," she said as she walked back in. She was obviously used to giving orders.

There were a few other people outside, at the other end of the patio. But Will and I were sitting alone. He was slouched in his wheelchair with his face tilted skyward. That's when it started.

For ages we just sat. Will didn't say a thing. I tried to think of something to say, something funny to make him laugh, but it was impossible. It was starting to get damp and depressing around us. Drops of mist were forming tiny puddles on the cold, white plastic chairs and tables. Most of the people at the other end of the patio had gone inside.

I was about to wheel Will back in when this strange thing happened. His eyelids were half-shut, like they'd been since the morning, but I could see this glimmer in his blue eyes. Will's eyes are a special blue, the color of denim. Honest. Just like your favorite old pair of jeans that you've worn so many times they feel just great when you put them on. Faded blue denim. Anyway, he was watching something intently.

I followed his gaze to the table between us, where I had my sneakers propped. An ant was struggling in a drop of water in the middle of the table. It was a prisoner, held by the water's tension, all six legs paddling helplessly.

I watched the ant with Will and thought about the hours we used to spend when we were little kids, lying on our stomachs with our magnifying glasses, just watching the ants. Little kids have lots of time for stuff like that. And the way those ants could carry things much heavier than they were. Fifty times heavier, in fact. We'd looked it up. And if they dropped something, they'd just pick it up again. Or if we put a twig in their path, they'd find some way around it. Persistent little things. Strong and persistent.

Anyway, I was thinking about all this and watching the ant, who was still struggling like crazy, when all of a sudden I heard Will scream. I looked up at him, but his eyes were still half-shut. His face was set like a mask. I knew he couldn't have done it, but somehow I'd heard him. "Free him!" That's what he'd screamed.

I touched the drop of water gently, just enough to break its tension. Off the ant went, all six legs working perfectly.

I glanced around to see if anyone was looking at us, but there was only one old man left on the patio and he was reading a newspaper.

No one else had noticed the ant. No one else had heard my brother scream.

Ms. Kirby appeared from nowhere, with a folded blanket tucked under her arm. "Wouldn't you rather wait inside for your parents?"

"No. We're fine out here. Honest. They'll be here soon. They're with the specialist now."

She nodded and tutted under her breath as she began adjusting the pillows in Will's wheelchair and tugging him under the arms. She managed to get him all nice and propped up with the blanket around his shoulders, but then he slowly started to slide back down again. I couldn't tell if he was doing it on purpose or not, but Kirby had another try. Back down he slid. Then it was her turn. She tugged and propped. He slid. It was like they were playing a game. Will was winning.

She was about to try again when I finally spoke up. "I think he'd rather slide down. He can see better when his head falls back. It's because he can't open his eyes all the way." Damn, I sounded like I was apologizing.

She looked at me. "I know, but he can't be comfortable slumped down like that. It's bad for his spine, you know. He'll have a terrible backache tonight." She patted the pillows that braced him. "You're more comfortable sitting up properly, aren't you, dear?"

I smiled to myself as I imagined what "dear" would tell A. Kirby, RN, if he could, but Will was barely talking now. He'd have said something that would sound very polite until she really thought about it. He'd have put the know-it-all in her place. But he'd say it so cleverly, she probably wouldn't get it. It would sail right over her starched white cap, too quick, too sharp for her.

But Will couldn't tell her off, and neither could I. I hated myself for being so helpless against her. So Kirby hoisted him more firmly, propping his head upright, then wheeled him like some kind of out-of-order robot away from me and nearer the edge of the patio.

"There, dear," she said, walking back toward me. "You're right, you know—the fresh air is best for him. And just look at the sky." She turned and stared at the sunset that had burned through the gray clouds. Then she seemed to remember something, glanced at her watch, and walked quickly back into the ward.

I moved the table and chairs over to Will. The sky was incredible—orange and pink crowding the pale gray. I hoped the sunset was a good omen. I needed a good omen right then as I looked at Will, propped up helplessly in his chair, staring down at his useless thighs.

I wanted to help him slide back down again so he could see the sky, but I was afraid Ms. Kirby would catch me and make a scene. I hate scenes.

Mom and Dad joined us with hot chocolate that burned your fingertips through those stupid thin plastic cups. You needed asbestos fingers to drink the stuff. Mom wrapped Will's in a napkin and kept blowing it before she dared hold it to his lips. And then it kept dribbling down his chin, where she'd catch it with a tissue.

Will, dribbling. I thought of making a joke about how Will would be even better at basketball, now that he could dribble so well. I knew Will would think it was funny, but I wasn't sure about Mom and Dad. They were trying to hide it, but I could tell they were worried. I wondered what Dr. Woodson had said to them.

Eventually, Mom stacked the empty cups up. "Can you two handle Will's chair? I think we ought to go inside now."

"Sure," I answered, happy for the chance to move around. I tucked the edges of the hospital blanket up around Will, and Dad helped lift as we clanked the chair

11

clumsily over the runner of the sliding glass door and into the ward.

Will hadn't been talking very much since we'd gotten him to the hospital. It seemed to be a big effort. And when he did talk, it was hard to understand what he was saying. He tried to look at us now through his half-closed eyes. His mouth opened and shut, helplessly, like a fish out of water, but there was no sound. Then his eyes shut tight and a tear squeezed from the outside corner of one. We all stood there frozen, watching as it traveled slowly over his cheekbone, stopping in the hollow. I couldn't remember the last time I'd seen Will cry.

Dad crouched down in front of the chair. "It's okay, Will. It's okay to cry, son." He looked up at Mom as she stroked Will's hair.

"You'll be all right, Will," Mom said.

I stared at the tear on his cheek and thought of the ant trapped in the drop of water. "Free him," Will had screamed, and I had. It had been easy.

Now Will was the ant. I reached for the tear and brushed it away. It felt cool on my thumb.

CHAPTER TWO

WE WERE ALL UP EARLY the next morning packing Will's backpack with some of his favorite stuff. It had never even been emptied from our vacation. No time yesterday.

Dad put in the portable game of chess. Mom chose a few books she thought she'd read to him, but they looked pretty boring to me.

I added the Walkman and all his best tapes. Oh yeah, and I dug out his old teddy bear, Indibadoo, from the attic and slipped it in. Indibadoo with his chewed ear and only one glass eye. I remembered when Mom had tried to sew .on a new eye. Will wouldn't let her. He said Indibadoo had lost it honorably and wouldn't want it replaced with a button.

Mom and I walked to the bus stop. Dad was following with the backpack later, in the car. He was phoning work to try to get an extension on a research project he was finishing up, so he'd have more time to be with Will.

We had to pass old Mr. Rawley's house. He was in the

front yard, sprinkling salt on slugs. That's the kind of thing he enjoys.

"Hear someone's in the hospital," he shouted at Mom. He always shouts.

"Yes. Our older son, William. We're on our way to see him now." I could tell Mom didn't want to stop and talk to him, but Mom's nice to everyone, even if they don't deserve it.

"What's he got? Broken bone from all that football and basketball, I guess." He was busy now with a pair of clippers, trimming the hell out of some poor scraggly bush. "By the way, someone's been cutting across my lawn on their bike." He glared at me.

"I'm awfully sorry, Mr. Rawley," Mom said. "We really have to go now. Please say hello to Mrs. Rawley for us." She started to walk away before he could answer, and I could tell from the sound of her high heels on the pavement that even she was fed up with Rawley.

"You mad, Mom?"

She turned to look at me and seemed sort of surprised. "Yes, I guess I am, Peter." She shifted her pocketbook to her other arm. "I'm angry. And sad. And even a little frightened. I think you probably are, too."

I nodded. "It's just so hard to believe. I mean, Will was fine and then all of a sudden . . ."

"I know. It's all happened so quickly. We've barely had time to talk." She reached for my hand as we walked. It felt weird. We hadn't held hands for a long time. I guess I'd decided it was kind of babyish. But it was okay to hold her hand now.

"This is going to be a hard time, Peter. Especially with both your father and me working."

"Yeah, I know. But we'll manage, Mom. Besides, school doesn't start for a while." I walked along, trying to miss stepping on the cracks in the sidewalk. It's a stupid habit I got into when I was younger.

Mom squeezed my hand and didn't say anything else as we caught our bus for the short ride to the hospital. I could see her chewing the inside of her mouth. She always does that when she's worried.

When we got to Will's room, he was in his wheelchair. He looked about the same as he had the day before.

"I've brought you some clean pajamas, Will. Peter, can you help me get him into bed? You get his top half, I'll lift his legs."

I moved the chair nearer the bed and slid my arms under his, but the chair began to roll and bumped Mom's legs.

"Wait a second, Peter. The brake's not holding." She fiddled with it. I could see a few gray hairs on top of her head. I hadn't noticed them before.

"It's such an old chair. The physical therapy department is trying to get a better one, one with a headrest, but goodness knows how long that will take. They said it could be months."

Alarms went off in my head. Months? How could she be talking about months? Will wouldn't need the stupid chair that long. My mind was racing, but I didn't want to say anything in front of Will.

"There, it's braced by the bed. Ready, Peter?" she said, grasping Will under the knees. "Lift."

I managed to get his torso onto the bed, but his legs hung helplessly off as Mom struggled with their weight. I started to help her.

Getting him into his pajamas wasn't easy, either. Will tried to cooperate, but his arms and legs felt heavy and useless.

"Let's see if Dad's here," I said when we'd finished. I nodded my head toward the hall and winked.

Mom looked puzzled.

"Come on," I said, winking again, slower.

"Oh yeah. Uh, be right back, Will," she said, tucking him in.

"Are you telling me everything, Mom?" I blurted out once we were in the hall. "I mean, what's all this about getting a new chair in months? Months! He won't need a chair by then. Heck, he's going to be out of that thing in days."

I waited for her to say something. "That's right, isn't it?" I asked. "He'll be walking long before that."

She frowned. "Of course that's what we hope. Why are you looking at me like that?"

"Because you don't sound too sure."

"Peter, the doctors aren't sure." She brushed a stray piece of hair off her forehead. "They're doing another test today. Then maybe we'll know more." She waited, but I had nothing to say. "I'll phone home now and see what's keeping your father."

I went back to Will's bed. He'd drifted off. I watched him sleeping and felt better. At least when he was sleeping, he still looked like Will.

I thought about all the times I'd watched him sleeping since we were little kids. We'd always shared a bedroom, and I was usually the first one up. I'd stare at him and try to wish him awake, so he'd get up and play with me. And it worked, too. One minute he'd be lying very still with his eyes shut tight; then suddenly he'd stretch and wake up, as if I'd touched him or whispered something in his ear. But I never had. I'd only wished he'd wake up.

I wanted to touch him now, but I was afraid he would feel cold and lifeless. His chest was barely rising and falling. It reminded me of when we were little and played soldiers. In the game, one soldier would pretend to be dead, trying to hold his breath or keep his chest from moving. If he did it well enough, the enemy soldier would think he was dead and try to take his weapon. Then the pretend-dead soldier would reach up and grab him. I wished Will would reach up and grab me now.

"You must be William's brother," a soft, sure voice interrupted my thoughts. "Do you call him William or Bill?"

A woman stood at the bottom of the bed, wearing a badge: ANNE MARTIN, PHYSICAL THERAPIST. "I'm Anne," she said. She held out her hand for me to shake. I did. She had a good grip, not like a dead fish.

"I call him Will," I said. "And I'm Pete."

"Well, I'll be visiting Will several times a day, as often as I can. We'll be doing passive exercises with him, keeping his body moving so that he doesn't get too stiff. Otherwise his tendons might shorten and he really would have problems when he starts to move again."

"When?" I asked. I hadn't planned to ask; I just blurted it out.

She looked up from her notebook, which was crammed with pieces of paper. "When what?"

I moved nearer to her. I didn't want Will to overhear, but I needed answers. "When will he walk again?" I lowered my voice and tried to sound cool, but my heart was beating really hard. "When will he sit up? When will his eyes open?" I looked at Will. He was still sleeping. "When will his damned body start working again?" I stepped back and felt as if I'd shaken her by the shoulders.

"I can't get through to your dad," Mom said as she came back to Will's bed and sat on the edge, between me and Anne. "It's busy."

Anne looked at me a moment and then started to introduce herself to Mom. Great, so one more person wasn't going to give me an answer. Was this a conspiracy?

"I was just about to do some exercises with Will. It might be useful for both of you to watch," she said. "Actually, you can help me, Pete. Will needs to do these exercises as often as he can. Okay?"

"Sure." So she definitely wasn't going to answer my questions either. Maybe no one knew the answers.

She leaned low and close to Will, whose eyes were now open. Her voice was quiet and confident. "I know you're tired, Will, but let's give this a try. These exercises are important. Let's go, okay?"

She was the first person I'd seen in the hospital who actually spoke to Will as if he had a brain and could understand.

"Will, are you in any discomfort?" she asked as she bent his arms gently.

Will moved his eyes slowly toward Anne's. It was like some big effort, just to move his eyes.

Will closed his eyes as Anne carefully bent the joints of his arms and legs. She did it slowly, but I could see she was working them hard.

"We'll have another try later, Will," she said in a low

voice, as if she didn't need to bother reassuring the rest of us. Will was the one that mattered.

Mom kissed Will good-bye and promised to come back after lunch. She was going in to work to explain about Will and try to get more time off to be with him. She kept smoothing his blanket and fluffing his pillow.

"It's okay, Mom," I said. "I can take care of him until you and Dad get back."

She smiled and looked relieved. "I know you can, Peter. Thanks." She gave Will one more kiss and left us alone.

The ward quieted down in the late morning, which was good because I needed to talk to Will. I wanted to ask him about what had happened the day before, when I'd heard him scream. I wanted to know if it was just me imagining things or if something really had happened.

I leaned close to his ear. He didn't smell like himself. His eyes were shut.

"Will. That ant. Did you want me to free him? Was that you shouting at me?"

I waited, hoping he would open his eyes. If he could just let me know. I felt like I could help him get free, too. Like the ant.

Then I heard the dreaded noise of Ms. Kirby. She made me really nervous. It felt like she was trying to get between Will and me. I started sweating. I worried she'd give me a hard time about something. I had no clever answers. No way to shut up her clanking cart.

I wanted to stand up to her the way Will would have. That's when I heard Will's voice. But this time he didn't scream. It was more like a laugh, a joke between the two of us, but clear as day: "Pajamas," he said.

Pajamas? Of course—our game. It was great when you were bored, but it also worked on the school bully, or just anyone who was giving you a hard time. Will was right. It would work on Kirby.

It sometimes took a second to imagine what someone might wear in the morning as they made some coffee or brushed their teeth. But if you could just picture them in their pajamas, it kind of made them harmless, funny even. Will called pajamas the great leveler.

I thought hard for a minute as I heard her footsteps. They squeaked. Then it hit me. Frilly, short, sexy pajamas. With those high-heeled slippers with feathers on the toes. Black ones.

I looked up at Ms. Kirby and suddenly saw her in the outfit I'd imagined. I couldn't help smiling.

She stood at the end of Will's bed with her hands on her hips. "What's the joke?" she asked.

I felt kind of sorry for her standing there in frilly short pajamas and black feather slippers. I just shrugged. I couldn't tell her *she* was the joke.

"It's time for your brother's test. I'm sorry, but you'll have to go now. Come back after lunch with your parents." Then she gathered the bathrobe around her—it was a red silk kimono—raised her chin, and marched off. A huge dragon smiled at me from her back.

"Got to go, Will," I whispered. "I'm hearing you, buddy. I'm sure of it. I only hope you can hear me." I stared hard at Will sleeping, and for a second it was the old Will I saw, laughing, making faces, his blue eyes full of mischief.

"I know you're still in there, Will. We'll get you free, buddy, whatever it takes."

CHAPTER THREE

EIGHT NEON TETRAS darted in perfect synchronization. Two enormous black-and-white angels turned and became impossibly thin. A big black loach fastened its vacuum-cleaner mouth to the side and hung on, ignoring the show-offs.

What a great old time waster the hospital aquarium was. I could have spent the whole day just sitting in front of it with Will. And the way things were going, it looked like we might be doing just that.

After three days in the hospital, Will was not getting better. In fact, he was getting worse. He could hardly wiggle a toe or finger now. The tests they'd done the day before had been positive, so at least they were sure what was wrong with him now. It had some foreign-sounding name that everyone pronounced differently. Mom wrote it down for me on a piece of paper. *Guillain-Barré.* She said it was French and pronounced *ghee-yan bah-ray.* I practiced it a few times. Mom was always asking lots of questions about the sickness, but there didn't seem to be many answers. Just that Will's paralysis was normal. Normal. Ha.

But we were settling into a kind of routine. Mom and I went to the hospital in the morning while Dad put in a few hours at work. Then they changed places so Mom could work.

The changeover left me about an hour alone with Will, just after lunch when it was quiet. I called it our time-out and made the T signal to tell Will we were alone, the coast was clear.

I stayed the whole day and even ate in the hospital cafeteria. I was trying every kind of grilled sandwich they had and was beginning to invent some new ones. Grilled cheese, baked beans, and pineapple. It's not bad. Honest.

The main thing was, we were there with Will, helping him do his exercises, reading to him, trying to keep him from being bored out of his mind.

So the hospital aquarium was just the thing, safely out of the reach of Ms. Kirby, at least for the half hour she allowed us to be off the floor. I'd positioned Will just right to see it, head back so he could watch the fish.

And the fish weren't the only thing to watch. This may sound strange, but I was amazed by how many sick people there were. From tiny babies to very old people, especially old ladies. Tons of old ladies. And when they weren't in their beds, they were usually wandering around the hospital in robes and slippers, lots of them holding on to metal walking frames. No need for the pajama game here. Usually people were buying candy and newspapers from the hospital gift shop. Or just killing time, like Will and me.

We were lucky to be in the lobby. They were nervous about Will leaving pediatrics at all. Kirby made him blow into a machine every hour to make sure he was breathing okay. But I still thought it was better for Will to move around. Some people never left their rooms, never even left their beds. That really depressed me. Must have depressed them, too.

Will slept a lot on our travels. Couldn't seem to get enough sleep, in fact. And he slept so soundly. Hospitals are really noisy places. Big old clanking beds could be rolled past us, and Will wouldn't notice.

I couldn't always tell when Will was sleeping, so I'd just keep on talking. Which wasn't very peculiar because I talk to myself a lot anyway.

"I wonder who takes care of you," I said to the big black loach with his mouth planted on the side of the fish tank. This was the first time I'd spoken to a fish. I started making faces at it. I act stupid a lot, especially when I'm by myself or bored. It amuses me. It drives Mom and Dad crazy sometimes, but Will usually likes it.

"Don't you get tired of hanging around the tank?" The loach just blinked at me. "Hey, that was a joke. Hanging around the tank—get it?"

"Fred's got no sense of humor. It's always been his problem."

I hadn't noticed the little man in the white uniform before. I felt kind of embarrassed, wondering how long he'd been listening to me being a moron.

Before I could think of anything to say, a little kid started crying in the gift shop. He'd spilled a whole bag of M&M's. They were rolling all over the place. His mom was yelling at him. The guy in white walked over to him and did this trick with his hands that looked like he was pulling off the end of his finger. I could see how he was doing it, but it was still pretty clever. The little kid loved it and stopped yelling. So did his mom.

Then this guy—I could see from his name tag that he was an orderly—swept up the mess and bought the kid a new bag of M&M's. Problem solved. Brilliant.

"Who takes care of the tank?" I asked as he joined us at the aquarium.

"Well, Fred here does most of the hard work. He keeps the tank clean. I give them a little food now and then."

"Yeah, Fred's a loach, isn't he?"

"That's right. You know about fish?"

"A little. Will and I were thinking of starting a tank once. This is Will, my brother."

It was kind of embarrassing introducing people to Will. He couldn't shake hands or say hello or anything. But this little guy didn't seem to mind. He just picked up Will's right hand and gave it a squeeze with his own two hands.

"My name's Edgar," he said. He bent down and looked right at Will. He didn't have to bend very far because he was so little.

"You haven't been in the hospital long, have you? I know nearly all the patients."

"It seems like ages, but it's only three days."

Edgar took a small can of fish food from behind the aquarium and eased the plastic lid off. Then he lifted up the top of the aquarium and crumbled a pinch of multicolored food into the water. A piece of it floated, but the tiny pieces sank. The fish all changed positions instantly, some diving, others surfacing.

One of the angels came right up to Edgar's small finger, which he'd dipped into the water. The fish seemed to nibble on it. Then Edgar did the most amazing thing. He stroked the fish near its enormous top fin. The fin went down, like a dog's ears when it's really getting into a good scratch. The angel made several more passes at Edgar's finger. Then he joined his mate.

"I never thought of petting a fish," I said. "I'm surprised they like it."

"They're a little like people," he explained, lowering the top. "Not all of them do." He bent slightly, his hands on his knees, so he was at eye level with the fish. He wrinkled his nose and peered into the tank. "Fish have personalities. If you and Will watch this tank enough, you'll see. Some of them are top feeders. Gulpers. Eager to get there first, get the most. Brave, really, like the angel. Seraphim, I call him."

The big angel was at the top, sure enough eating the bigger pieces of food that were still floating.

"Others are more cautious. They wait their chance. They're bottom feeders. Patient. They let the food dissolve and trickle down. Less risk that way."

I watched, and he was right. They were either at the top or the bottom. The brave and the cautious. Just like people.

I tried to decide what kind I was. Easy. A cautious one who waited at the bottom. Will was a top feeder, a leader.

"Are your mom and dad able to come and visit much?" Edgar asked.

"Yeah, they take turns because both of them work. But Dad is at home on his computer a lot of the time anyway."

"What does your dad do?"

"He's an anthropologist. He teaches at the university, but he loves to do fieldwork when he can."

Edgar raised his eyebrows. "Sounds great. You boys ever get to travel with him?"

"Sometimes. If it's during vacation. We just got back from five weeks in England," I said. "But that wasn't work."

"No." Edgar laughed. "Sounds more like fun to me. I'll bet your dad brings back some interesting things from his travels."

I smiled, thinking of some of the outrageous stuff Dad has lugged back over the years, things that filled our house and made it look like no one else's. Giant calabashes, hyenas' teeth, bronze carvings, tapestries, huge leather hassocks.

"That's for sure. Last time he came back, he had a clay water pot that I could nearly fit into."

"And what will you do with that? I guess it would be useful if there were a drought."

"Mom will find something to do with it. Somehow everything Dad brings home finds a place and a use."

"So he's a collector."

"Yeah, his special thing is masks. He has masks from all over the world. They cover the walls of his office. Now they're spilling out into the rest of the house. Mom says we're running out of walls."

As we talked, I'd kept one eye on Will. He was breathing kind of fast, like he was out of breath. And he kept sliding down in his wheelchair even worse than usual. It was almost as if he was trying to get my attention.

"Think I ought to get Will back to his room now. Ms.

Kirby said no more than half an hour." I glanced at my watch. We'd been gone close to an hour.

"Okeydokey," Edgar said. "I'll see you boys later on, maybe back here at Fred's place, eh?" He gave us a wink and hurried off, whistling something or other. He kind of reminded me of the White Rabbit in *Alice in Wonderland*, usually in a rush to get somewhere.

I got Will back up to his room and settled in his bed. Luckily, Kirby hadn't noticed we were late.

I started doing some of the exercises with him that Anne Martin had shown us, bending his arms and legs, pushing his feet back to make sure the tendons in his legs didn't shorten. I got this feeling again that he wanted to tell me something. His eyelids were kind of fluttering.

"Is something in your eye, Will?"

He stopped blinking and stared hard at me with his blue denims.

"Think," I kept whispering to myself. "Think what he wants, dummy. He's trying to tell you something."

He started blinking again. First he did it fast. Then slow. Then fast again. Three fast. Three slow. Three fast. Again, three fast, three slow, three fast.

Then it hit me. Morse code. Will was blinking SOS! Three shorts, *S*. Three longs, *O*. Three more shorts, *S*.

"I'm reading you, Will: SOS. You want to use code. Jeez, I hope I can remember. I know I should after all those nights we tapped our messages in bed. I'll try, Will. Talk to me."

Will stopped blinking SOS. He closed his eyes twice, slowly.

I was racking my brain. "Two longs, two longs," I whispered. "What the heck's two longs? *G*? No, that's two longs and a short." Then I remembered. *"M!"*

Will closed his eyes. I couldn't tell if he was agreeing with me or just plain exhausted by my stupidity. But then he opened his eyes and started again. This time it was a short and a long.

"That's easy, pal. *A*. So we've got *M-A*. Great going, Will. Give me another!"

I could almost smell Kirby—she was getting really close. Will had his eyes shut again, but this time he wasn't opening them.

I grabbed his shoulders. "Wake up, Will. Kirby's going to kick me out in a minute. Tell me the next letter."

Slowly, painfully slowly, his eyes opened. They seemed to take forever to focus.

"You've exhausted him," Kirby snapped. "I told you half an hour. You'll have to leave now and let him rest."

At the sound of her voice, Will's eyes closed.

"But he was okay. We were just watching the fish. Honest. He was breathing fine." I was desperate for the last of Will's message. "Ms. Kirby," I started, getting up from the bed, "Will was using Morse code with me—you know, blinking his eyes to give me a message."

She smiled and shook her head slightly.

"Honest. He really blinked two letters. Isn't that terrific? He can talk!"

Kirby picked up his chart. "I'll make a note of it, but I'm afraid you'll have to let your brother rest now. A hospital is run on schedules. Without schedules and routine, things would come to a screeching halt. Do I make myself clear?"

I nodded, not daring to irritate her even more. She had the power.

I felt frustrated but happy. Will was spelling with his eyes. His isolation was broken. As I rode my bike home, I was talking to myself, as usual, saying all the *M-A* words I could think of. *Macho, macadamia, macaw, machete*? I laughed; a machete might be useful on old Kirby. No, too bloody on her white uniform. *Macintosh, Martians*? My bike was pedaling itself.

CHAPTER FOUR

"HE'S GORGEOUS-LOOKING, isn't he?"

"Shh, Claire, he'll hear you. He can hear, can't he?"

"Course he can. Have you seen the color of his eyes? I've never seen eyes like them."

"What do you mean? I heard he couldn't open his eyes."

"He can. A little bit. But even so, you can see they are this wonderful blue. And with his dark hair and all."

"Too bad he's so thin."

"He wasn't this thin when he came in. It's muscle atrophy. He can hardly move at all. Has to be turned over every twenty minutes or so. Ms. Kirby says he's in a lot of discomfort, but he never complains."

"Well, how can he? He can't talk."

"No, but Anne Martin has been trying to think of a way to help him to communicate. Millie, can you tighten your side of this bottom sheet?"

"Hey, what's this?"

"Oh, his brother brought that in as a joke. It's his old

teddy bear. His family's great, you know; his parents take turns coming to read to him and help him with his exercises. But his brother's the best. He spends the whole day with him, talking and joking. Gets him out of the ward, too, when Ms. Kirby allows it. His brother's gorgeous, too. Have you seen him?"

"Honestly, Claire, he's only a kid. Sh, here comes Ms. Kirby."

"I don't think this patient requires both of you at the moment, Miss Jacobs."

"It's just that there was nothing else to do, so I thought I'd help Claire—I mean, Miss MacDonald."

"Miss Jacobs, there is always something else to do in pediatrics. There is never a single minute when our services are not required in at least three places simultaneously. Now, please see that all the water pitchers are filled with fresh water, and don't ever let me hear you say that there is nothing else to do again. Is that clear?"

"Yes, Ms. Kirby."

"Good. Now, Miss MacDonald, has this patient been turned in the last twenty minutes?"

"No, Ms. Kirby; we were just about to do that."

"Turning a patient can easily be accomplished by one able-bodied person. You are able-bodied, aren't you, Miss MacDonald?"

"Yes, Ms. Kirby."

"Good. Then turn this patient onto his stomach. Make sure his ankles aren't crossed under the covers. Then check that there are bedpans in each table. There have been complaints. I'll be in central supply."

"Yes, Ms. Kirby."

I hadn't been eavesdropping exactly, but I couldn't help

hearing the discussions by Will's bed as I sat on the patio just outside his room. The curtain at the huge window was closed because the sun was so bright, so they didn't know I was there. I waited until all was quiet; then I went in to see Will.

The curtains were pulled around his bed. Perfect.

"Hey, Will, you awake? I've got something for you. Open your eyes, buddy."

His eyelids twitched slightly as if invisible strings were tugging at them. They finally opened enough for me to see a little blue. I positioned myself on the bed so he could see me. "Time-out, Will," I said, making the T sign. "We're all alone, and I've got plans for you.

"You had me up half the night trying to figure out what you were spelling. *M-A, M-A* kept going through my mind." I moved closer to Will, watching for any reaction.

"First I thought of Mom's macaroni."

No reaction.

"You're not really too hungry these days, are you? Then I guessed *matches* until I remembered you don't smoke."

A slight twitch.

"Then I concentrated. I started thinking about what I'd want if I were stuck in your body right now. I'd want to escape, just like that ant the other day. Remember, Will? Yeah, I'm sure you do. I thought of the game we used to play when we were little kids. Our special game."

I had him now. A spark in the blue.

"It's been ages since we played the game."

I thought back to the day, the two of us sneaking into our dad's office. The enormous wall, covered with his collection. And how badly we wanted to take one down and try it on, just once.

" 'Hold the chair while I climb on it,' you said. It was a swivel chair, and you crashed to the floor. I'll never forget Dad's face. And how we all ended up on his office floor laughing.

"And do you remember what Dad told us that day? The story about how he had started his collection, the places he'd visited. The weird things he'd seen and heard of."

I thought back to that afternoon, the three of us hunched in the corner of his office, the rain beating down outside. It had been the first time I'd ever heard Dad talk about his work as an anthropologist.

"Remember the stories? The transformations. The medicine man who became a leopard. The old woman who changed into an owl."

I looked down at the thing I had brought for my brother. I felt its power in my hands. There was danger, too, with this power. Dad had warned us. "Magic has consequences," he'd said. "And sometimes the consequences are unexpected." But I couldn't think about that now.

I put it down and took Will's hand in my two. "Can you squeeze my hand, buddy? You don't have to make me say uncle or anything; just a little squeeze?"

I squeezed his hand and closed my eyes and waited. I don't know what I expected, but I concentrated as hard as I could, wanting to feel any sort of movement. Finally, I thought I could feel the slightest kind of twitch. Like when you hold a baby bird in your hand and it's so scared it doesn't dare move but sometimes it can't help it.

"You know what I think, Will? I think you've kind of forgotten what movement is like. Your brain doesn't know what to tell your muscles to do anymore. Hey, like that time we spent most of the summer vacation learning how to wiggle our ears. Remember? We used to spend hours in front of the mirror, flaring our nostrils, raising our eyebrows, but our brains didn't know what to tell our ears to do."

I laughed to myself. "But we both got it finally. You were first and tried every way you could think of to explain to me how it felt, how to make my ears perform the trick. And I just sat there and I thought really hard about the muscle right in front of my ears and I pictured my ears moving up and down, up and down. And when I finally did it, it seemed so natural and easy. We wiggled our ears so much that summer, Mom said she thought they were going to fall off.

"I'm wiggling mine now, just thinking about it. Anyway, the point is, I think your brain has forgotten how to tell your muscles to move. It needs a refresher course. I think you heard me and Edgar talking about Dad's masks at the aquarium. That's what gave you the idea, wasn't it, Will? Yeah, I'm sure of it. So I've brought you what you wanted, Will."

I held the mask in front of his eyes.

"Will, you know what this can help you to do, don't you? It can free your soul, your spirit." I leaned closer to my brother to whisper the secret that he already knew. "It can free your body, Will."

I fitted the mask carefully over his face, making sure his eyes were behind the holes, his mouth lined up with the mask's. I had no special words in mind, no mystical incantations. We'd never needed those before. All we'd needed was our belief.

I thought again about what Dad had told us, how a mask is not something you just hide behind, but something that can transform you. I felt frightened for a second and shivered. Some scary memory kept trying to surface in my mind, like a deep-sea monster. I wasn't sure exactly what I was getting into. But I knew I had to put my fear behind me. Will wanted this. It was the one thing I could do for him.

"I spent a long time deciding which one to bring you. There are so many. I tried to choose one Dad wouldn't miss, but he's thinking about you too much to notice anyway. I thought the bat might be fun, flying around in the night and all. Then the frog seemed like a good idea, all that leaping around. But in the end there was only one. Like the man says, you have to crawl before you can walk.

"You're on your stomach, Will. Low to the ground, actually rubbing on it. You're looking for something. I don't know what. But you just sit still. You're trying to get somewhere, Will, carrying a load on your back, moving slowly. You're not out to break any speed records, but you're moving. Remember how it feels."

I stood up and looked through the eyeholes of the mask to see Will's drowsy lids. Perfect, I thought, taking both his hands in mine and picturing the scene in my head.

"Are you afraid? 'Cause I am. I think it's okay to be afraid, Will. We're together."

I concentrated even harder, thinking about a box turtle that we'd watched one really hot summer, crawling toward a pond. I stared into Will's denim eyes and began to feel slightly dizzy. I held his hands even tighter. "It's happening," I whispered. "Become the turtle, buddy."

Congratulations, brother! A hospital full of high-tech machines and specialists, and only you can figure out what the hell is happening with me. I have so much to tell you, Pete.

I feel like hell. Worse than I've ever felt. Tired and uncomfortable. And I can't complain. But I have you, Pete. You're the big brother now. It's all up to you.

Hey, Pedro, I can feel it. It's working! Man, I'm feeling peculiar. Way down in the pit of my stomach, in that network of nerves. What's it called? Oh yeah, the solar plexus. That's where the change is starting. It's making me feel dizzy, like I'm sort of levitating off the bed. No, I'm not. I'm on the ground. I'm in some tall weeds, so I can't see much, but I can smell all kinds of things around me. I'd like to just sit here, but I have to move.

Jeez, I'm thirsty.

I have to find water. I'm crawling along, slowly, unbelievably slowly, through hollow brown reeds. I can smell the water that used to be here.

I stretch my neck to see how far I've come. I've hardly moved. Behind me there is a path of flattened reeds, as if something has been dragged. It's my shell! No wonder it's such hard going. This thing's heavy, but I don't have far to go. I can smell the water, wet and cool and fresh. Waiting, just for me.

In a minute or two I'll lower my head at the edge and stretch my neck. My thick tongue can almost taste the water, chilled by the night air.

Wait a second. What's this noise? Behind me dry grass

is crackling as it gets crushed. Something is panting and excited, short of breath.

It's stepping on me, but I don't think it's trying to break my shell. It's prodding me with a wet nose, like a puppy's, soft and moist. But jeez, its claws are sharp.

The thing is quick and it's moving around the back of me, darting in and out, nipping at my feet and tail. I can't see it without sticking my neck right out, but I don't dare.

I'm scared, Pete. Maybe this wasn't such a hot idea. I can feel my heart pounding deep in my shell. If only my heart could make my legs move faster, so I could run for it. No chance. Not with this damned shell.

That's it! My shell! I don't have to run. I hiss and pull my legs, tail, and head in. I even lever up the hinge of my shell. Tight. Tighter. I'm a little locked box that no one's got the key to.

It's dark in here. And close. Do box turtles get claustrophobia? I won't think about that.

The thing is swatting at me now. I guess it's frustrated. It's batting me around on the grass. I'm spinning like a top. Oh, I get it, this is a game. Now I'm rolling. I can't even tell if I'm on my back. Do I dare open up? Maybe just a crack.

Damn. Big mistake. A small sharp claw is digging in the crack, trying to get me out. Right, pal. I'll tighten my shell and close the crack. It's hard, but I've done it. What now? The stupid animal has got its claw stuck. It's yelping. So. I've trapped the hunter. But now I'm being dragged and I'm definitely on my back.

I have to open my hinge the tiniest bit. That's done it.

The claw is out. The thing, it must be a dog, is yelping, but it's running away, disappearing into the rustling grass.

I'm alone again, but there's a big problem now. I'm right beside the cool, clear water, but I'm on my back again. Damn.

Any suggestions, Pete? Guess I'll wait. Maybe, if I'm very slow and cautious, I can open my hinge slightly. I'm peering through the crack. There it is. I can see the water. I am that close.

I'm pushing my head out of the folds of skin that protect it. A little like putting on a sweater. Seems safe enough. Okay, legs, your turn now. They're reaching for the ground, but where the heck is it? I'm stretching my head to one side on its long leathery neck, pressing hard on the grass. It's hot and dry and smells funny, like the animal who was playing ball with me.

Hold on, I think I'm just about to turn over. . . . Damn. I've slid farther down the bank.

Tell you what, I'm exhausted. Think I'll pull my head and legs partly in; it's getting real hot out there. In here, too. I'm starting to feel desperate, Pete. I want to turn over, to be on my stomach. Upside down is no way to be, especially for a turtle. Not if he plans to last long, anyway.

I'm dying for a drink.

All right. One more try. I've got to try again. If I'm this thirsty, there will be others thirsty, too. And they'll come to the water to drink. And hunt.

I'm arching my neck for all I'm worth. I can feel my hard shell almost cutting into my skin. The legs on one side are pushing until, jeez, I think they're tearing away from my body. My claws are scraping at the ground. I can feel the weight struggling to shift in my shell. Just a little more. I'm pushing again, so hard that my legs are trembling.

I'm going to close my eyes and push until there's no push left. My shell is teetering. Go on, you traitor, get over.

It worked!

I snap my legs and head into my shell as I flop over. I'm going to wait on the inside, safe, listening. No sounds. Only the pond. It sounds like it's licking the dry earth at its edge.

I'm ready. I'm opening my hinge and peering out. My eyes feel so dry, so tired. But I'm here. I'm going to drink. But hold on. There are voices, far off.

I pull myself back in and wait. It's hard to wait, but sometimes it's better. The water will still be there.

I know I'll make it now.

"Just look at his covers."

"They're a mess."

The two nursing assistants looked at me accusingly as I peered through the curtain at Will.

"You two been having a pillow fight?" the one called Claire asked playfully.

"No. Honest," I said, amazed as they were at the sight of Will's bed. "I've been on the patio, uh, reading." I knew I didn't sound at all convincing, but waved a library book as evidence. "Is Will okay?"

I looked down at his exhausted body. I could only guess what had happened to him, if anything, while he'd worn the turtle mask. I had been by his side most of the time and couldn't see much of anything happening. Some twitches in his arms and legs. Some sweating. But he'd only had it on for a minute or two. Then I'd thought I heard the clinking bottles of Ms. Kirby, so I'd left Will and walked out to the hall to see. Sure enough, it was her. I couldn't think of what to say, so I just started talking to her about what things Will liked to eat. I was really going around in circles, and she finally got tired of listening and left with her cart.

When I got back, Claire and Millie were already at Will's bedside. I couldn't see the mask anywhere.

I tried to accept that the magic hadn't worked this time. I looked down at his poor, tired body and realized it might never work.

"Seems more like a water fight, if you ask me," Millie interrupted my thoughts. "Or maybe he knocked his water pitcher. His pillow's soaked."

"No. His pitcher's still full, just like I left it. I've only been gone twenty-five minutes," Claire added, examining her watch, just like Ms. Kirby. "Besides, he can't move; how the heck could he spill his water?"

"Hold on a minute—this isn't water. It's sweat. You can smell it." Millie was sniffing Will's soaked pillow. "We'll have to change his sheets," she said, pulling his blanket down. "But he doesn't feel feverish now," she added, feeling his forehead. "We'd better call Ms. Kirby."

"No. Wait," Claire interrupted, panic in her voice. "There's something else different. I'm sure I left him on his back. Oh, my God, I was supposed to turn him over. I forgot."

"Don't be silly. You must have done it. He's certainly not on his back now."

"I'm telling you, I forgot. Something must have distracted me. You don't think Ms. Kirby turned him, do you? I'm in for it."

"She couldn't have. She left here and went straight to central supply. As far as I know, she's still there."

"Then how?" They both looked at me, the question hanging in the air.

It had worked! Will had moved! I shrugged, trying to wipe the silly smile off my face. "Maybe he got tired of waiting and just flipped himself over."

"What's this?" Millie reached under the bed and held up the turtle mask.

I shrugged. "It's mine. I'm going to a costume party." Pretty pathetic, but it was all I could think of.

Millie eyed the mask. "As a turtle?"

I smiled weakly and put the mask into my backpack.

Ms. Kirby clattered into view just then. "Has he been turned?" Man, she made him sound like a hamburger.

"Yes, he's on his stomach now," Claire said timidly.

"Miss MacDonald, he was on his back when I left him. You were about to turn him onto his stomach then." She looked at her watch. "According to my calculations, he should be on his back again."

I glanced at the hamburger. He was fast asleep and probably wouldn't mind being turned again, so I headed down the hall to the coffee shop. For some reason I was dying for a drink.

CHAPTER FIVE

THE NEXT MORNING when I woke up, it was a second or two before I remembered. Will had moved! Only five days in the hospital, and he had moved. I lay in bed thinking about it, trying to decide who to tell. But then I thought, it wasn't up to me to tell at all. It was Will who had done it, and I didn't want to steal his thunder. So I'd let Will tell them, or at least show them. He could do his Morse code trick for them, too. Everything would be different today.

I went down the stairs three at a time and found Mom and Dad getting ready to leave for the hospital. We were all going to meet with Will's specialist, Dr. Woodson. Anne Martin would be there, too. Together they would decide how Will was doing.

"What's that humming?" Dad asked at breakfast.

I shrugged my shoulders.

"Why, it was you, Peter. You were humming," Mom said. Then she took a sip of her tea and looked at me over the edge of her cup, like she was trying to figure something out. "You always hum when you have a secret. You've done it since you were a little boy."

"Have I?" I kept eating my cereal and pretended to read the boring stuff on the back of the box.

"Peter, you're still humming." Mom was smiling. At least she hadn't forgotten how. "Want to let us in on the secret?"

"You'll find out soon enough. Can we leave for the hospital now?"

I couldn't wait for them to see for themselves how Will was doing. I couldn't wait for everyone to see the improvement. Especially Dad. It was weird, but Dad seemed to be having the hardest time accepting Will's illness. I'd heard them talking during the night, when I was in bed. Dad kept asking why Will was so sick, asking Mom if she thought it had anything to do with the traveling. He sounded guilty, like he was somehow to blame. He just couldn't deal with it. I really wanted Dad to see Will move.

When we got to the pediatrics unit, Dr. Woodson and Anne Martin were already there.

Mom stood next to Will's bed and took his hand in hers. I wondered if she could feel his strength coming back. Dad stood at the bottom of the bed with his hands in his pockets.

It was kind of eerie with us all gathered around Will's bed, as if some weird ritual was about to happen. In a way, it was. Anne pulled the curtain around all of us, cocooning us from the rest of the room.

First, Dr. Woodson told us what he was going to do, how he was going to test Will's reflexes. It irritated me because he spoke to everyone but Will, the poor guy he was going to do it to.

He peered over his glasses at Will and took this tiny hammer out of his pocket. First he picked up Will's arms, then his legs, as he tapped his elbows, knees, and ankles. It was kind of funny to watch him tap-tapping with his tiny silver hammer. Reminded me of a story Dad used to read us about the elves who made shoes for the old shoemaker while he slept. I wondered if Will thought of that.

Dr. Woodson kept shaking his head slightly and tapping some more and frowning at Will as if he wasn't doing it quite right. Finally he sighed. "He's not responding," he said to Anne, tucking the little silver hammer into his breast pocket. He made it sound as if it was Will's fault.

Then he moved down to the end of the bed and uncovered Will's feet. Without giving Will any warning, he ran his thumbnail up the sole of one of his feet. From the heel right to the toes. It made me jump.

Everybody looked at me, and I laughed. "Sorry."

Dr. Woodson peered over his glasses at Dad. "If this is making the boy uncomfortable, perhaps he should wait outside."

"No," I said. "That's okay. I'll be fine."

Mom took hold of my hand and gave it a little squeeze. I squeezed back.

Dr. Woodson did the same thing to the other foot. My toes curled in my sneakers, but I didn't move. Neither did Will.

Finally Dr. Woodson stopped and looked at Anne.

It was her turn. She tested his muscle strength at this time every day, but only I knew she'd get a surprise today.

I was getting really excited. Forget his stupid reflexes as long as his muscles were coming back. I was impatient and cocky as I looked at Mom's and Dad's hopeless faces. I moved to where Will could see me.

"I'm pretty sure he's getting stronger," I blurted out.

Anne looked at me, and a deep line shot between her eyebrows. "It's pretty early, Pete," she said. "Don't expect too much, okay?"

"Sure." She'd seen right through me. "It's just that, uh, yesterday his fingers seemed to move a bit." I was dying to tell her that he'd flipped himself over in bed. And about the Morse code. But I wanted Will to show her.

She looked hard at me, and I could tell she was trying to hide her disbelief, but it was there, in the crease between her eyes. "Well. Let's check it out." She smiled at Will and talked to him as she gently arranged him on the bed. "Are you awake, Will? Time to earn your keep."

Will's drowsy eyes hardly opened.

"Sorry to put you through this, Will, but I need to keep track of how you're doing. Okay?" Anne leaned down and tried to peer into the narrow slit of Will's eyes.

"Okay. Pete, can you help me prop Will up a little bit? Scoot that pillow underneath here. That's fine."

I helped her lift Will's back and shoved an extra pillow behind him so that he was nearly sitting up. His head lolled back on the pillows and his body seemed incredibly heavy as we moved him, almost as if he was fighting us.

"Good. Now, Will, can you move your right leg at all for me?"

We waited. Nothing happened.

"How about your left leg, then? Can you move that one?"

Still nothing. Mom and Dad kept looking at each other.

"Well, maybe we're being a bit ambitious. What do you think he moved yesterday, Pete, his fingers?"

"Yes."

Anne took his right hand and gently laid it on the bed, palm up. "Can you manage to wiggle your fingers, Will?"

Nothing. Not a damn thing. His hand looked like a dead crab.

"Come on, Will. Show them what you can do. Don't make me a liar." I tried to sound jokey, but my throat felt tight.

Mom was standing where Will couldn't see her, biting her lower lip. Dad was fumbling to get out through the opening in the curtain, like a frightened kid in a school play. He stopped as we all heard voices and commotion on the other side of the curtain.

A new kid had been admitted a few hours ago. Just below the gray curtain I could see a bed's wheels and two pairs of shoes, probably the mom's and dad's. They were standing near the bed.

"This is going to be a piece of cake," the dad was saying. "And just think of the great story you'll have to tell your pals when you're back at school."

"I think he's having an appendectomy," Anne Martin explained as the bed clanked out of the room and the shoes disappeared.

I suddenly felt very angry. An appendectomy. That kid would probably be back with his friends, just like his dad told him, in no time. While Will had to lie here getting worse and worse. It was so unfair. I could see from Dad's face that he was thinking the very same thing.

"Look," Anne said, "this isn't very nice for any of you, least of all Will. But I have to tell you, this is to be expected. Will may continue to weaken." She looked helplessly at Dr. Woodson.

"That's right," Dr. Woodson agreed. "My initial diagnosis has proven correct. The paralysis could well spread."

Maybe it was just me, but it sounded like he was pleased with himself for getting it right. It just wasn't important what the damned diagnosis really meant to Will. As far as I was concerned, Woodson had ice in his veins.

Anne moved to the side of the bed, near Mom. "But this is the important thing," she said, rubbing Will's limp hand. "This is the thing we all have to remember, especially you, Will. When the weakening stops, you'll get better." She looked at Mom for a long time.

The whole time, the Iceman kept polishing his Ben Franklin glasses. I wanted to throw them on the floor and step on them.

He finally suggested that we all sit down with a cup of coffee and give William a little rest. Just what he needs, I thought, a rest.

We went down to the cafeteria, and I tuned out while Woodson talked about Will's condition. It all sounded like a textbook, anyway. He said things like, "in cases such as these" and "according to the literature," and it was as if he wasn't even talking about my brother.

I just kept sipping my Coke and staring at the tiles on the floor, trying to make sense of it. Why was this happening to our family? To Will? And how the heck could he manage to turn himself over in bed yesterday, and today not be able even to wiggle his fingers?

I got really mad when Woodson said it would be better if we left Will alone to sleep for a few hours. "The examination would have exhausted him," Woodson said.

"Can't I just hang around?" I asked. "I won't bother him; I promise."

But it was no use. You'd have thought I wanted to take Will discoing or something, the way they acted.

I thought about Will all the way home in the car, about how unfair the whole thing was. I kept hearing Woodson's monotone voice and seeing him scrape his damned thumbnail up Will's foot.

Meanwhile Mom and Dad talked quietly in the front seat. They had the radio on. I could hear their voices, lowered, talking, talking, always in low voices unless they spoke to me. Then their voices were louder and brimming over with fake cheerfulness. It made me sick. Didn't they think I could handle it? Didn't they know that I wasn't a little kid anymore?

At lunch I could tell they were trying to make things seem normal, as if we were a real family again. They kept asking me lots of questions about sports and friends and the coming school year. I tried to answer them, but it all seemed so pointless. Who cared about any of that now? All I wanted was to get back to the hospital, to be with Will.

Then Dad lowered the boom. I knew it was coming, but I couldn't duck. "Pete, your mother and I think maybe you've been spending too much time at the hospital."

He waited, but I didn't say anything.

"The specialist pointed out that Will might continue for some time like this before he starts to improve. But that's the main thing, Pete, the thing we have to hang on to: Your brother's going to get better. But in the meantime . . ." He paused here and took a drink.

I still didn't say anything. I wasn't going to make it easy for him.

"In the meantime, we've got to carry on with our lives as well as we can." It was Mom talking now. This had obviously been rehearsed.

That was it. That was the sort of comment I'd been waiting for. "Is Will getting on with his life? Is he, Mom?"

"Try to be reasonable, Peter. This isn't easy for any of us."

"I am trying, but what's reasonable about what's happened to Will? Why couldn't he just have broken his arm or got appendicitis? I can't make any sense out of someone perfectly strong and normal being turned into a zombie."

I didn't care if my words hurt. I wanted them to. How could they want me to leave Will?

"Dr. Woodson said that when Will stops getting weaker, he'll reach a plateau for a while. Then he'll need us even more, to help with the physical side of things."

"The physical side?" I let the words hang. "What about the other side, Dad?"

Mom and Dad exchanged one of their looks. A look that said, "We're in this together." A real parent look.

"What exactly do you mean, Peter?" Mom asked.

I knew then that it was hopeless. They couldn't see beyond the skin and bones in Will's bed. The physical side was all. Forget the mind, the spirit. I couldn't believe it. Dad, who had told us all those great stories about the power of the spirit.

It really was all up to me. They didn't have a clue. "Never mind. It's not important. May I be excused?" I said as I got up from the table.

"Where are you going, Peter?" Mom asked.

"Back to the hospital."

Dad wiped his mouth with his napkin and threw it down on his plate. "Have you been listening to us?"

"Sure," I said. "I know. I only want to go back for my library book. It's due today," I lied.

"Right. Get your book, drop it off at the library, and come right back."

I left them at the table and went to Dad's office. I knew the mask I wanted. I grabbed it and looked at the empty place on the wall. It was right in the middle, above his desk. Too obvious. So I took another mask down, one near the corner of the room, and stuck it in its place.

I managed to get into the unit without bumping into Kirby or Woodson, and no one else was very interested in me. It was our usual time-out just after lunch. The ward was nice and quiet. Will was lying on his side, one leg raised and a pillow supporting his back so he wouldn't roll over. His eyes were slightly open and he was staring at a light across the room.

"Can you still do the code, Will?"

He shut his eyes for a long time, which I thought meant no. I couldn't tell if he was too tired or if he just couldn't pull it off anymore. I knew that I had to continue, to try the mask again.

"This is going to have to be quick, Will. They think I'm spending too much time here. Sick joke, huh? And you know what else they say? They say you're getting weaker,

Will, but I know better. Oh, sure, you look a little weedy now, but I know inside, where it counts, you're strong."

His eyes moved to me.

"And angry, too. You're so strong and angry you'd like to tear this whole damned unit apart."

A glimmer.

"Not just the unit—the whole shitty hospital. Am I right, Will? Are you angry?"

A glint.

I pressed the mask onto his face and studied the heavy brow. I could see Will's dazed eyes through the deep-set holes.

"Try this on for size, buddy. You're king of the castle now. You've got a real nasty attitude. You're a big, mean, hairy, don't-mess-with-me gorilla. You're so red-hot angry, you could even melt that iceman, Woodson, with a look. So flex those muscles, pal. Take the whole damned world apart."

You've got it, Pete: I'm angry. Yeah, I'm totally pissed off with getting weaker and weaker. But you don't know the half of it. You see, they talk over my body—visitors to the ward, sometimes even the nurses. They talk as if I can't understand. As if I'm brain-dead. Don't they think I know about how my breathing is getting worse, every time I blow into their damned machine? I can hear them talking about permanent nerve damage. About how some guy died of this. Heart failure. Yeah, I lie here and I take it all in and I think about it. That's all I have to do, Pete. Think.

So now I'll think about this gorilla. You didn't say where I am this time, Pete. Shall I just let the mask take me where it wants? I'm getting that peculiar feeling again. Way down in the solar plexus. That lighter-than-air, floaty, kind of scary feeling.

Yeah. Now it's happening. Now I'm feeling very big and strong. I'm squatting on the ground. I'm this big, powerful coiled spring just waiting to let go.

But hold on. Who dares touch the king? Someone with nimble fingers is picking at my back, searching in my coarse brown hair, finding an insect and pulling it away gently, careful not to pull the hair itself. It feels wonderful.

Know who it reminds me of, Pete? Kirby. But you don't know about Kirby and her secret back rubs, do you, Pete? In the middle of the night, when everybody else is asleep or busy, I lie here and feel like I'm going to explode. You see, Pete, it feels like there are tiny insects crawling around under my skin and I can't scratch them or swat them or do any damned thing about them.

But Kirby knows. Somehow she knows. And she rubs my back and my legs and arms. She makes the insects go away.

Just like someone is doing now to me, the gorilla. So you see, I don't feel particularly angry at the moment. In fact, I'm feeling really peaceful.

I'm looking at my finger. It's like dark brown leather. A ladybug is crawling onto it from the ground. When I hold my finger in the air, she does an about-face and crawls up again. I could watch her all day, crawling for the highest point. I remember the game we played, telling them to fly away home. So much for the big hairy beast, eh, Pete? Sorry, pal.

But what's this noise? Afraid someone's rattling my cage, Pete. I'm a zoo gorilla, you see. There's this crowd of people watching from the other side of the bars. They're shouting things, making fun of me, I think. Maybe they saw my ladybug. Trying to get a rise out of the king. One of them has a stick he's running along the bars.

Should I rise to the bait or just ignore the idiots? My ladybug has flown away. I turn toward the crowd and stare my angriest tiny-eyed, heavy-browed stare. That shuts a few of them up, anyway.

But the hard core still taunt. A younger gorilla, one who doesn't have a silver back like mine, runs to the bars. The crowd shrieks and scatters. He drums his chest and shakes the bars. His shaking makes a terrible racket.

But his anger can't break the bars.

And anger won't make me better, Pete. Let it go.

▧▧▧▧▧

I'd sat beside Will for the few minutes he'd worn the mask. The curtain was pulled around us. Nothing much had happened. Will hadn't moved. The magic hadn't worked this time.

I could hear the kid who'd had the appendectomy being wheeled back into the room. He was asleep and his mom and dad were waiting for him to wake up, talking to him.

I listened. They sounded so happy, so relieved to have him back. They seemed like a nice family.

I took the mask off Will's face. His eyes opened slowly. He looked really peaceful.

I pulled open the curtain, and a strange thing happened. A ladybug flew into the room and landed on Will's bed.

It looked so bright and cheerful on the white sheet. I watched as it climbed onto Will's finger. I thought it might bother him and I tried to get it to crawl onto mine, but it just kept turning around, going back to Will.

After a while I found my library book and said good-bye to Will. The ladybug was still there on his finger, as if it were attached by an invisible thread.

CHAPTER SIX

"ANIMALS HAVE no place in a hospital. I won't allow it. Not in the pediatrics unit."

Boredom, like a woolen blanket, was smothering the unit. The children, stuck in their beds or able only to wander around a small area, were bored stiff. They looked out of the windows at the hot summer day or just lay sadly in their beds, wanting to do all the things kids do when the sun shines.

Ms. Kirby crashed through the boredom like a one-man band. She ground her medical cart to a clattering halt and shook a toilet brush and bedpan in the air, banging one on the other. I couldn't believe it. The racket was incredible.

"Where is it? Where is that wretched bird? Open all the curtains and windows, Edgar. Wide open. Let that bird out and the fresh air in."

Kids' voices from the floor could be heard shouting above the noise.

"It was here, Ms. Kirby, just inside the window."

"I saw it going into the bathroom."

"Frances gave it her bowl of Jell-O."

"I did not. And anyway, he wouldn't eat it. Too wobbly."

The parade came into our room and was growing like one of those crazy dances where everybody grabs the waist of the person in front of them and they all snake around the room.

Excited kids were screeching and laughing. Everyone was looking under their beds, in closets. Even Edgar was in on the act.

"Have you seen it?" Ms. Kirby demanded.

I shrugged my shoulders. "Seen what?"

"That filthy, verminy thing. Strutting around like it owns the place. No doubt excreting everywhere it goes."

I looked at Edgar, who followed Kirby, holding an empty pillowcase. "A pigeon," he explained, then winked.

"What's excreting?" one of the smaller kids shouted at Ms. Kirby.

She pursed her lips. "Pooping."

The kids loved this, and cries of "Pigeon poop!" could be heard up and down the unit.

Mom and I were doing passive exercises with Will, ones where we bent his arms and legs, forcing them to stretch. But this was too good to miss, so I loaded him into his wheelchair and joined the search.

It was wonderful. Kids who had been lying around on their beds for days, pale and miserable, suddenly had a reason to get up and run around. One or two in wheelchairs were tearing up and down the hall, shouting, "Pigeon patrol!" and nearly colliding with the staff.

I think I even saw Ms. Kirby smiling as she disappeared beneath a bed, whisking a feather duster under it and calling, "Here, pigeon, pigeon." Honest.

Claire and Millie made sure everyone was included in the fun, searching under sheets and pillows of the kids who couldn't get out of bed, tickling them with hidden feathers. It was the first time I'd heard so much laughter in the place.

I was amazed that Kirby was allowing all the commotion. In fact, she was not only allowing it, she was the ringleader.

"Whew," she said as she finally collapsed in a chair. Her starched cap was cockeyed. "I think we got rid of it, don't you, Edgar?"

"Yes. At least for now," Edgar agreed. "Never know when she might come back, though." Then he did an incredible thing. He winked at Ms. Kirby. What nerve, I thought. Amazing.

And even more amazing, Ms. Kirby winked back.

A warm breeze traveled through pediatrics, blowing temperature charts and old newspapers as the excitement of the morning quieted down. Children were busy drawing pictures of the mystery pigeon to hang above their beds.

"Was there really a pigeon?" I asked Edgar when he came back to our room to close a few windows.

"Course there was. My friend Matilda."

"Huh?"

"Matilda. My pigeon. She wanders into the hospital now and then. Always livens things up. You should have seen the surgical ward last month. She had them in stitches." He grimaced. "Oops, sorry."

He smiled his funny little side-smile, shrugged, and began whistling as he struggled to pull the heavy curtains across the glass doors.

I laughed. Old Edgar was quite a character. He seemed to be everywhere in the hospital at once, always busy, always in the know. But he still had time for you. He knew the names of all the kids in pediatrics and he'd bring them little surprises, stuff people had made or donated to the hospital. He loved playing Santa Claus.

Edgar sat down on the edge of Will's bed. He had to hoist himself slightly, and when he got up there he looked like a kid. His feet dangled high above the green tiles.

"Where's your mom? The noise too much for her?"

"No. She loved it," I said. "She's just getting us some cold drinks."

"And how's it going with Will? I haven't seen you two at the aquarium for a while."

"No, we've been hanging around the room mostly. Will's a little weaker every day, but Anne says that's normal."

"Must be rough on you and your parents, though. Watching."

I shrugged. "I'd change places with him if I could."

Edgar nodded. "Sure. It's the worst part of caring for sick people. Just waiting and watching helplessly."

"Doesn't seem to bother some people," I said as Ms. Kirby called from the next room.

"Edgar? Where are you, for goodness' sake? I need help moving this bed."

"Coming," he called.

"How do you stand her, bossing everyone around?"

"Aw, she's not so bad."

"But why does she fuss around with her medical cart and bedpans and make the nursing assistants' lives miserable?"

"Because those are things she can control. She can make sure her patients get their medicine on time and she can take their temperatures and pulses and straighten up their beds. She can even make sure her staff do the same. That part of the show she can run, and mostly she runs it well."

He hopped down from Will's bed and smoothed the sheets. "But there are things she can't control."

"You mean like when patients get worse or die?"

"That's right. Things can go wrong. They do sometimes, even in pediatrics. And when they do, some people can just shake their heads and walk away from it. But not Althea, uh, Ms. Kirby. She takes it personally."

He leaned over Will's bed and whispered. "So don't let her fool you. She cares about Will. All of us do."

We both looked down at Will, who was asleep, curled on his side.

"Did he enjoy Matilda?" Edgar asked.

"I think so. It's hard to tell what's going on in his mind these days."

A new thought struck me. "Say, Edgar, you seem to know quite a lot about animals, I mean with your fish and pigeon and all. If you could turn into an animal, just for a little while, which one would you like to be?"

He wrinkled his forehead. I knew he'd treat the question seriously, not like most grown-ups.

"That's a very interesting question, Pete. I'd have to think about it for a while."

"What if you were Will?" I persisted. "Which one would you want to be then?"

"I'd have to know more about him. What does he like? Sports? Reading?"

I thought. How could I describe Will to someone who'd only known him in a wheelchair? "Will is like this: If he's never done something before, he's always willing to try it, no matter what. And when he does it, he's good." There was a word for Will. "He's a natural."

"A natural, eh? And now this has happened." He looked at Will and smiled his crooked smile. "If I were Will, I think I'd want to cut loose. You know what I mean? Do crazy things for the first time, for the sheer fun of it." He scratched his head. "You know those sort of monkeys. They come from Asia, somewhere in the rain forest, I think. Their arms are even longer than their legs and they are incredible athletes. They swing all over the place."

I thought about this, picturing the wildlife films I'd seen on TV. "Gibbons?"

"Edgar?" Kirby closing in.

He snapped his fingers. "That's it. I've got to go now. See you later, Pete." He started to leave. "Oh, almost forgot. I found something for Will. You might like it, too." He handed me a rolled-up poster. "Stick this up where your brother can see it." And he was off down the hall, whistling.

I unrolled the poster. It was one that had been popular years ago—a kitten, clinging by its claws to the very edge of something, its legs dangling helplessly. "Hang in there," I read out the caption as I stuck it on the wall within Will's view.

"Good advice, eh, Will? Guess that's what we're doing anyhow, just hanging in there."

I propped him up so he could see the poster.

"What do you think of Edgar's idea, Will? A gibbon. Sounds good to me. I think Dad's got one."

Mom came back with some cold drinks and held one to Will's lips. He couldn't even manage to suck through a straw. It took forever to feed him his mostly liquid diet, but Mom never lost her cool.

"Think I'll go home for lunch today," I said.

Mom looked surprised. "What's the matter? Fed up with the grilled cheese sandwiches?" She laughed.

"Think I've about run out of combinations," I said. "They've refused to make grilled cheese with marshmallows and ketchup," I joked. "Besides, I want to get some different tapes for Will. I'll leave now and come back as soon as I've eaten."

"There's no rush, Peter. Your dad will be here in another hour or so."

"I know. But I want Will to have these tapes. I'll see you later at the house. Okay?"

I rode home on my bike and didn't bother to eat. Instead, I went to the office and found the gibbon mask. It was one Dad had brought back from Borneo. Its small face was a perfect circle and had a pale ring around it. Its lips were drawn back, and it had long teeth, like a dog's.

I quickly rearranged the masks on the wall to make the missing one less obvious.

I got back to the hospital just at the right time. The lunch cart was gone, and most of the patients were dozing. Kirby was off the floor, so most of the nursing assistants were watching some soap opera in the playroom.

I pulled the curtain around us and gave Will the T sign and showed him the mask.

"Dad had a great story about this one. Remember? He

had to trade a dozen rolls of color film for it. And the next time he saw the film, it had been pulled out of its spools and wound around the arms, legs, and body of a witch doctor. Jeez, what a waste of good film. But then the picture Dad took of the guy was great.

"Anyway, time's a-wasting, Will. Take a trip to Borneo. Like Edgar says, cut loose."

<hr>

Jeez, it's working quick now, Pete. I hardly have to think at all. Even before you get the mask on me.

I'm high. Higher than I ever thought I'd be. I'm sitting right on top of the whole world. No kidding—there's a rainbow underneath me.

Everything is glistening and sparkling around me. Remember how it used to look when we walked to school in the fall after a heavy dew, how all the spiders' webs hung with droplets like tiny prisms that broke the light into colors? Well, I'm in the middle of the web. It's pure magic, Pete. Vines hang all around me, like sparkling necklaces. A giant's treasure.

I'm shaking a vine now, and the jewels are tumbling to the forest floor, breaking up, multiplying as they hit enormous plants.

I'm listening now, closing my eyes, to try to separate the noises around me—the hisses and chirps, screams and grunts. There is a loud cheeping near me, and I can trace it to an emerald beetle hiding deep inside the black center of the petals of a hibiscus that's redder than blood. All that noise, from one tiny bug.

I could explore this place forever, Pete, but I'm up here

to cut loose. On behalf of you and Edgar, of course. So what do I do? I know, I'll pull at the vine again and test its strength. It leads across to the next tree. I'm wrapping my long, leathery fingers around it. It feels like a hairy snake. I'm standing now, right on the edge of the branch, ready to swing. Okay, Pedro, here goes nothing.

Jeez, this is great. I'm swinging from vine to vine, just like on the monkey bars, but better, much better. I never stop moving. It feels so great to move like this. I'm dancing the rain-forest dance, Pete, a living pendulum that's swung right off its clock. Gravity? What's that? Oh, Edgar, you were right. I could spend the rest of my life doing this. But hold on, there's even more I can do.

I'm a tightrope walker, too. I'm no ordinary monkey, you know. And never mind water: I can walk on air. I'm standing up now, and my elastic arms are so long my knuckles actually brush the branch beneath me. I'm swinging my arms in huge circles, the world's greatest soccer goalie. Borneo's hope for the World Cup.

I jerk hard on the hairy vine at my feet. It shakes the trees, and all kinds of noises echo through the rain forest. I grasp the vine and my toes tighten like fingers. I'm going to walk across the empty sky between the trees. And the funny thing is, it's not scary. My balance is perfect.

I'll start out slowly, just to get the feel of it. Okay, now I'm going faster. Man, it's even easier going faster. I'm running now for the last few steps. Now a big leap and . . . whew, I've made it. Superb. Ten out of ten from the Borneo judge.

Anne would have loved that one. Poor Anne who can't even get a twitch out of me, if she could only see me now. Even Ms. Kirby would be impressed.

I can just picture her up here, waiting for me in the next tree. Me Tarzan, her Althea. No medical carts up here, Althea. No little upside-down watches. No need.

Hey, Pete, tell you who I would like up here in my private paradise. Claire. Think you could arrange that, Pedro? Could you slip a mask on Claire when she's busy taking my pulse or something? She'd make a lovely lady gibbon.

But back to reality. My reality, anyway. You can keep yours. I'm going to swing right around the canopy this time. One great big circle just to let them know I'm here. No need to test all these vines. Tarzan never tested the vines, did he?

Okay, Edgar, this one's for you. I'm off. And I'm going to "hang in there" just like the poster says. I feel like rapping, too. I'm going to rap my way around the rain forest. *Swing and snatch. Swing and snatch. In this forest I have no match. Feeling good. Feeling fine. Feeling the rhythm through the vine. Let go of one, another one's there, let go of that one, I don't care. I don't care if I never stop, just want to dance that rain-forest bop. Just got to dance that rain-forest—*

"Stop! Jeez, Will, you're killing my hand. It's me. Pete. Wake up! Let go of my hand. Kirby's on the ward!"

I'd been holding Will's hand for a few minutes when I heard the approaching clatter of Kirby. All of a sudden he started squeezing for all he was worth. It really was like the old days of playing uncle, but I had to get Will back to normal before the dragon got wind of what we were up to.

I looked down at him, and his eyes behind the gibbon

mask were wide open and startled, like a cat caught in the headlights. Honest. But I could tell he wasn't taking anything in. He was breathing hard and shallow, like old man Rawley when he tries to catch us cutting across his lawn.

Clunk, clunk, tinkle, tinkle was getting nearer.

I reached to pull the mask off with my left hand.

"Jeez, Will, let go. You're killing my hand," I half laughed, trying to pry his fingers off mine. It was like one of those death grips you read about. Only Will wasn't dead. Far from it.

I got the mask off and stuck it on my lap under the bed just before Kirby rolled up. Will's eyes had closed now, and I wondered for a second if I'd imagined it all, but I knew I hadn't because he still held my hand like a vise. I tried to think of what was going on in his mind. His grip was so desperate. Our hands were locked together, like two spiders in a fight until death. I pulled a corner of the sheet over them.

"Everything in order here?" Ms. Kirby wanted to know.

I nodded. In order? No, very much out of order. Wonderfully out of order. But nothing to worry about, Althea. Not yet, anyway. My fingertips were throbbing. Circulation was now completely blocked.

Kirby stood with her hands on her hips, like a general checking out the troops. She sighed deeply and pursed her thin lips. Lots of tiny lines appeared above her mouth in a neat, straight file. She stared at the bed.

"What are you holding under the sheet, Peter?"

I felt like a little kid who's been caught with his hand in the cookie jar. And my answer was about as cool as the little kid's would have been. "Nothing."

65

"Come on, now," she said, marching over to the bed. "There's obviously something going on here." She lifted the sheet, and we both looked at Will's hand clutching mine.

"Extraordinary," she said. "How long has he been doing that?"

"Oh, just a few minutes." Okay, the jig was up. "But don't you think it's a good sign, Ms. Kirby? Don't you think he might be getting better?"

She stared at me and looked kind of sad. "I don't know. I'll make a note of it and ask Anne Martin. It's very likely a muscle spasm," she explained. "Involuntary." Then she made a note on his chart and clattered off.

Involuntary, hell, I thought. I was trying to figure out how to make him let go when Edgar reappeared, rolling a large, clanking bed.

"Hey, Edgar, can you come here a minute?"

"What on earth?" he said as he looked at our hands, still locked.

"Kirby says it's an involuntary muscle spasm."

Edgar felt Will's fingers, testing their strength. He whistled under his breath. "Seems pretty voluntary to me. Like he's hanging on for dear life. One way to find out."

Then he did something very smart. He pulled Will's other hand from under the sheet. It was limp.

"Grab this hand with your other one and hold it tight," he said. Meanwhile, he pried open the fingers of the clutching hand. Immediately when the one hand was loosened, the other one gripped.

Edgar and I looked at each other. His eyes were all sparkly, and he was grinning like a Cheshire cat. "You know what I think, Pete? I think your brother is 'hanging in there.' "

I glanced at the poster. Edgar was right.

"It's okay, Will. I understand. You're hanging on to something. But you're here now, safe in your bed with me. You're holding my hand, but it's okay to let go, when you want to."

I sat watching his face. It never changed, but very slowly his hand relaxed.

I let go of it and leaned back in my chair, trying to figure out exactly what was going on. Was it Edgar's poster that had triggered the reaction, or was it the gibbon mask? I began to realize that I was playing with something that I didn't really understand. Like a little kid with matches. Trouble was, if anyone got burned, it would be Will. I needed help on this one.

Then it happened. The gibbon mask slid off my lap and onto the floor by Edgar's feet.

Edgar's mouth hung open as he stared first at the mask, then at Will.

In the darkened room, a tiny light went on.

"Edgar," I whispered, "do you believe in magic?"

CHAPTER SEVEN

"I CALL IT the great white beast." Edgar winked.

I looked at the ugly thing squatting on huge claw feet. It sat alone in the room, big and empty, like an animal waiting to be fed.

"What do you think, Will?" Edgar asked. I liked the way Edgar always talked to Will, just like I did. "It's no Olympic-sized swimming pool, but this old tub should hold you. You can float in it. They call it hydrotherapy."

"Hydrotherapy?" I asked.

"Yeah, I read all about it last night."

When work was slow or Edgar was off duty, he spent most of his time reading. People donated lots of books to the hospital library, and Edgar loved reading about everything.

"Hydrotherapy means using water as a treatment. It'll make Will weightless and take all the strain off his muscles. Anne Martin thinks it's a great idea."

It sounded good to me, too. Mom had left the hospital,

and Dad would be coming for his time with Will in about an hour. So it was our special time-out. But today we'd share it with Edgar. He was even giving up his lunch hour to help out.

"Will loves the water," I told Edgar. "In fact, Mom says he swam before he walked. But what about Ms. Kirby?"

"Anne Martin and I cleared it with her. As long as I stay with you and we're careful about his breathing, we have her blessing. They're so busy on the floor today, I think she's glad to have one less patient anyway."

"Great. Let's fill it up."

Edgar put the plug in and turned the large, old-fashioned tap. Water spluttered out, a trickle at first; then it gushed. The room was soon full of steam.

Edgar sat on the edge of the tub, stirring it with his hand. "I've been thinking about the masks, Pete. And about what you asked me yesterday, if I believed in magic."

I had wondered when he was going to bring it up. I'd tried to explain to him about the masks yesterday, but I had trouble getting it across. Maybe my vocabulary wasn't big enough. Or maybe talking about magic, real magic, isn't possible. It's like you take the magic away when you talk about it. I don't know, but that's how it felt to me.

"Did you play the game when you were little? Is that how it started?"

"Yeah. When we were really young. We got the masks down off the wall in Dad's office. I can remember holding hands and staring into each other's eyes through the eyeholes in the masks. But I can't remember the actual adventures. I think I was too young." I reached down and felt the water. It was just right. "It's odd because

I've been dreaming about them lately. I'm sure Will remembers."

I glanced up at Will, but he was nodding off in the steamy warmth. He was in his bathing suit, wrapped up in a white hospital blanket.

"And do you still play the game? I mean, even before Will's illness?"

"No."

"Any reason?"

I thought. "I'm not sure. Maybe we just got tired of it. Or just outgrew it. I can't really say."

"Do your parents know you're doing it now?"

I shook my head. "No, but I have to be careful. Dad noticed one of the masks out of place and asked Mom if she'd been dusting his office again. He hates it when she cleans his office." I laughed.

Edgar looked worried.

"You won't tell them, will you? I'm being really careful about the masks."

Edgar shook his head. "But what do you think the masks are doing? I mean, do you really believe they're helping?"

I watched his hand swirl the bathwater and thought about my answer. It wasn't an easy question. "I'm not sure, but they seem to be doing something. I think the turtle mask caused Will to turn over in bed. And after the gorilla mask he seemed much calmer. And you saw his grip after the gibbon mask—"

"And what about you?" Edgar interrupted.

"Me?"

"Yeah. Do you think the masks are doing anything for you?"

This was even tougher. Were they? I stopped to think. Was that one reason I didn't want Dad to find out about the masks and make me stop? "Yeah, I guess they are doing something for me. They're making me feel closer to Will, like I'm helping him." I shrugged and glanced at Will lying there looking so helpless. Will, who'd always won the trophies, always been the best.

"It's kind of hard to explain. I know the hospital staff are doing what they can for him, but that's not enough. They're only worried about his muscles and reflexes, his breathing and his heart."

Edgar laughed. "Those are pretty important things to be worried about."

"Sure. I know. But there's other stuff. Like, did you know there's energy flowing all around the body?"

Edgar bent over and turned the taps off. "Go on."

I was getting frustrated again. I was so bad at explaining it. I was pacing back and forth. "Well, you can't see this energy, but we know it's there."

"Yeah, I'll buy that."

"So, what else can't we see? What other things need to be taken care of when someone is sick? I don't know the exact words for it. I don't think you can just try to cure one part of a person and ignore the rest."

Edgar smiled and wiped the steam off his glasses.

"I know it sounds stupid. . . ."

He held his hands up. "Far from it, pal. You ever heard of Plato?"

"Sure. The Greek guy."

"That's the one. You know what he said? He said, and I quote, 'The part can never be well unless the whole is well!' "

"That's it! That's what I'm saying. Plato. And I always thought I'd never understand any of those guys."

Edgar laughed. "We'd better get Will in here while it's nice and warm. Is the raft ready?"

"Yeah. I've only put a little air in it, just enough to cushion Will and keep him afloat."

"Great. Is Will ready?"

"Yeah. He's got his trunks on under the blanket." I looked at Will, and his eyes were open.

I put the raft into the warm water. Then I got Will under the knees while Edgar had him under the arms.

"One, two, three, lift," Edgar said.

Will felt incredibly light. Horribly light. I could have lifted him myself. As we lowered him gently onto the raft, Edgar's great white beast swallowed him whole. His body weight caused the raft to sink just below the surface of the water.

"Perr-fect," I said.

Edgar agreed.

It was depressing to see Will's body as it floated on the raft. Most of his muscle was gone. That must be why he felt so light. Anne Martin told me muscle weighs twice as much as fat. And I guess I'd been building up my own muscles, lifting and exercising him. What's the saying— use it or lose it. Will was proof. But I tried not to think about that. I tried to think of all the things we could do together to get that muscle back on, once he really started moving again.

Edgar sat on one side of the bathtub and I was on the other. Our voices echoed around the high-ceilinged room as we talked to Will, encouraging him to try to move.

I did all the exercises with him that Anne had taught

me. I moved his arms and legs and stretched his tendons. I kept testing him to see if any strength was coming back. I talked to him the whole time. In fact, I almost forgot Edgar was there. We had such a routine now. I could imagine how it was for Will. Sometimes, if I pushed too hard on his leg, I could almost feel *my* hamstring complaining. I knew that being touched, being moved was important.

When we'd finished the exercises, I ran my hand through the water beside him. This caused the raft to rock a little, so that Will floated above it sometimes, not even touching it. It was the first time in days that Will's body hadn't been supported by something solid. I thought it must feel wonderful.

Edgar and I made slightly bigger waves, and Will's body slid up and down the tub, like a sea animal caught in the tide.

I swear I could almost hear him laughing, just the way he did when we were at the beach and he threw himself into the water.

"Surf's up!" Edgar said, winking.

"Go with the flow, Will," I added.

Let me lie in these warm waters forever. Let them wash over this tired body, this nightmare mind. Let me be a small sea creature that drifts with the tide, washed onto the shore, pulled out from the shore. Let me float, let me glide, let me sink and then rise, let me aimlessly drift in the warmth.

Pete, it's getting easier and easier to slip into the adven-

ture. I'm not sure I even need the mask. But you know what's hard? Coming back. I hate it when it ends. It's like coming back to prison.

I heard you talking to Edgar. You've forgotten about the danger, Pete. About why Dad stopped us from playing with the masks. It was so long ago, maybe you were too little to remember. But I remember. I can still feel the teeth on my neck, the warm blood. . . . But I can't think about that. Not now. I need to play our game again. Nuts to the danger.

You're really in charge now, Pete. Do you know that I'm in your hands? But I'm not worried, because you're strong, a lot stronger than you know. I hope someday you realize how strong you are.

I can feel your hand as you pull it through the water, making the waves. This steamy bath is wonderful, but I can go somewhere even better. I'm going to try to get there all on my own, Pete. No hands, no eyes. No masks.

I'm floating somewhere in warm, tropical waters. I'm free and moving with the tides, just below the surface of this incredible aquamarine world. Around me are tiny fish, each one more outrageous than the last. I feel shapeless and colorless. I am a jellyfish.

Giant purple clams, yellow sea anemones, orange star-fish. Every shade of every color. Fish wearing stripes, dots, gaudy carnival costumes. Or more sedate, camouflaged sand dwellers. Life is all around me, but it's freakier, more fantastic in this underwater spectacle.

And yet this world exists, silently, right next to our own air-breathing gravity-heavy world. How can this be? And what about other worlds then? There can be more. Is death

just a trip to another world? Can I go there and come back again? Would I want to come back?

The tide is shifting, dragging me out. I can feel the water turning cold as I move deeper and deeper. The gentle waves have stopped. It's calm and cold and I'm being pulled down. Down. Oh, I'm afraid. I'm getting heavy. It hurts. It hurts.

"The plug's out."

"Yeah. The raft must have caught it. The water level's way down."

"I think we should get him out now anyway. The water's getting cold."

"We could fill it up again if you want," Edgar suggested.

I looked at Will. "No. He wants to come out."

Edgar looked at me. "You seem sure."

I laughed. "I am." It was true. "Okay, I can manage him if you get the blanket opened on his chair. Ready?"

I lifted Will into his chair and wrapped a giant towel and the blanket around him. He was sleeping like a baby.

"We'd better get him back to the ward," Edgar said. "It's time for lunch."

"Yeah, Dad will be here soon." I was rubbing Will's hands and feet. "Thanks for helping us, Edgar. That was great."

"Do you think Will enjoyed it?" he asked.

"I know he did," I said. "Couldn't you hear him laughing?"

Edgar shook his head. "No, but I believe you could. By

the way, Pete," Edgar said, wiping his glasses, "the answer to your question is yes."

"Huh?"

"I do believe in magic."

CHAPTER EIGHT

THE NEXT DAY was Mom's birthday. Dad had insisted that she take some time away from the hospital. It was hard convincing her, but she finally agreed to have her hair done and do some shopping. Then Dad was going to take her out to dinner. They both needed the break.

Dad and I had been at the hospital since after breakfast. We'd been playing a game of chess next to Will's bed. It was Dad's idea. Will couldn't play, but at least he could watch.

Dad still had trouble with the whole thing. I noticed that whenever Anne came to test Will's strength, Dad always found a reason to leave the room. But he was doing his best.

Claire and Millie interrupted our game as they wheeled a cart into our room.

"We've decided Will needs a new hairstyle," Claire announced, putting on a plastic apron. "Is it okay with you, Mr. Chisholm, if we give him a shampoo and haircut?"

Dad said, "Great idea. It'll be a nice surprise for my wife. Today's her birthday. She'd been wanting to ask about it herself, but she's not too handy with scissors."

I laughed. "Remember when she decided to economize and cut our hair? She stuck a bowl on my head. Remember?"

Dad held up his hand, laughing, too. "Don't remind me. Go ahead, Claire. You have my blessing."

I looked at Will. His hair was greasy. Shaggy, too. Lying around in bed for days doesn't do much for your looks.

"I leave him in your capable hands," Dad said. "Bye, Will. Mom and I will be back later." He ruffled Will's hair. It was strange the way Dad touched him. It was like he thought Will might break. "Maybe you should get out on your bike for a while," he said to me. "It's such a nice day."

"Sure, Dad. Maybe later." We'd had a sort of truce since they'd told me I was spending too much time with Will. I tried to be cool, to seem less intense about Will, and they didn't make such a big deal about me being with him most of the day. And I lay low when the Iceman came for his daily visits.

I watched now as Claire expertly washed his hair, managing to soap it twice and rinse it thoroughly with barely a drop splashed on the bed. Then she combed it gently, getting rid of the knots. "Okay," she said, standing back and admiring her work, "it's your turn, Millie."

"I was training to be a beautician," Millie explained, snapping the air with her scissors. "But I decided a medical career was more glamorous." Pretty sarcastic, old Millie. "This place needs some atmosphere." She took a pocket radio off of the cart and tuned in a rock station. Turning it up, she began to work on Will.

I watched her, fascinated, as she began, letting Will's hair fall into its natural part, trimming a bit here, a bit there. "A man should never look like he needs a haircut." She spoke with authority. "But he shouldn't look like he's just had one, either."

I had to admit, when she'd finished, Will looked quite a lot better.

"Bet his girlfriend won't know him," Claire said, admiring Millie's work.

"He doesn't have a girlfriend," I said. "At least, not at the moment."

Claire and Millie exchanged a quick look. "What about you?" Millie asked. "Bet you've got a girl."

"Uh-uh."

"You want to do the nails or the facial?" Millie asked.

Claire screwed her mouth to one side. "Better stick to the nails," she said. "I've never done a facial."

"Right."

We loaded Will into his chair, and Millie stood behind him. While Claire trimmed his nails, Millie put this warm towel over his face. She never stopped talking the whole time she worked. Guess she learned that at beauty school, too.

"Opening the pores," she informed me. A few minutes later, she took the towel off and rubbed some cream into her hands. She began with Will's forehead and slowly massaged the skin over his eyebrows in tiny, circular strokes. She moved down his face, over his cheeks and nose, down to his chin. It looked so relaxing, I almost fell asleep watching.

"Time for some sun," Claire said as they put their stuff away. "Can you wheel him out, Peter?"

We propped Will further up in his chair, and I pushed him over the frame of the sliding glass door and out into the incredibly strong sunshine. It really was a terrific day. I hoped Mom was enjoying it.

Claire and Millie trundled their cart away, rolling and laughing down the hall, sounding like two girls on a carnival ride.

I realized as I lay in the sunshine next to Will how my attitude toward the hospital had changed. At first, I'd hated it. The cold echoes. The awful mixture of disinfectant, antiseptic, and sick people. All plastic and stainless steel. Time divided and subdivided by mornings with Mom, afternoons with Dad. And our special time-out sessions. And by Kirby's schedule. The constant noise of carts— medical carts, meal carts. Beds always being moved around. Life on wheels, but definitely in the slow lane, clanking around the hospital, going nowhere, crossing off the days.

But somehow the pattern and repetition had become comforting. It got so that I preferred the hospital to home. I would have slept there if they'd let me. Honest. Like a monk in a narrow bed in a white and antiseptic room. The hospital, the pediatric unit, Kirby, Edgar, Anne, Claire, and Millie—they were the real world. The outside world was just one I had to get by in until I could get back to the hospital. Back to Will.

I'd stopped seeing my friends. A lot of them were still off on summer vacations anyway. But if I bumped into one of them on my way to or from the hospital on my mountain bike, it was always the same. They'd heard some vague, confused story about Will and they would ask a bunch of questions, most of which I couldn't answer, so I'd just put on this fakey cheerful front. But I knew they could see right through me. Mom says I'm transparent. It was better just to avoid them.

But there were some people I couldn't avoid, like Mr. Rawley. Creepy Rawley, the kids call him. He's one miserable old codger, Rawley—the kind of man who, if you accidentally kicked your soccer ball into his garden, would read you the riot act before giving you your ball back.

He'd always catch me on my way past on my bike. He'd scurry out of his front door like a spider who's felt a shudder in his web, all morbid and craving bad news. Scuttle. Scuttle. I'd have to stop and talk to him. Not talk, really. Just answer the questions he fired at me. I hated passing his house. So did Mom. But avoiding it would have made the trip to the hospital even longer.

Then this morning I'd had a great idea. A way to handle old Rawley. The E game, Will and I call it. When someone asks you yes-no questions, you answer them "yes" if the last word of their question included an *e* and "no" if it didn't. It makes no difference what they actually ask. All that matters is the *e*. The game had worked like a charm.

Rawley: "How's your brother? What's his name—Ben?"

Me: (Ben has an *e*, so that answer is yes.) "That's right."

Rawley: "Guess he'll be in the hospital for a long time, eh?"

Me: "A long time. Yes, he probably will."

Rawley: "Not likely to pass it on, is he?"

Me: (Loving it.) "Yes, it's possible."

Rawley: (Retreating two steps.) "Well, what are they doing? Drugs? Surgery?"

81

Me: "Yes. Surgery."

Rawley: (Gaining enthusiasm, practically rubbing his hands together, like a fly on a fresh cowpat.) "Where exactly is the problem? The head? The heart?"

Me: (Perfect, I thought.) "Yes, both actually."

Rawley: (Nearly drooling.) "Gracious me. Bad luck." (Then, in a fakey, reverent tone:) "And is he expected to recover?"

Me: (Taking my time, hating to end his fun.)

Rawley: "I mean, is he likely to be left a, um, vegetable?"

Me: (A solemn nod.)

Rawley: "That's rough. A cabbage, eh?"

Me: "Yeah. Maybe." (I paused here and leaned forward to squeeze my front tire, which looked a little flat, trying to think of another *e* vegetable. I wasn't playing strictly by the rules now, but I couldn't help myself.) "He might even become a lettuce or an eggplant." I thought a minute. "Maybe even a beet," I added helpfully as I pedaled off. Two *e*'s. Well done.

I doubt Rawley will ever bother me or Mom again. I might even slow down when I go past his house, but I bet he won't run out. Sad, really.

I glanced over at Will. The sun had become very hot. "Hey, Will. You're catching flies, buddy."

Will's mouth was hanging open. He was even starting to drool a little bit. I got up and blotted the corner of his mouth with my cuff. "Not too cool, Will." I laughed, pushing his chin up with my finger. A minute later it was open again. His eyes seemed more closed, but I could tell he was awake. I pressed his mouth shut again, and this time he closed his teeth around his lower lip, holding his mouth shut. I felt kind of sick. Will's face was becoming more paralyzed.

In fact, even with his haircut and all, he still looked pretty awful. His body, which had been mainly muscle, was now mainly bone. His color was like someone who'd got a quick vacation tan and then been stuck in an office for days—that fading, sickly yellow.

My mind went back to Rawley and the vegetable thing. I felt guilty for even joking about something so awful. I tried to think of something to cheer myself up. I was no use to Will depressed. I took the mask out of the plastic bag. It was a heavy one. I stared at it. A peacock. It seemed like a sick joke now. But then, as I thought about it, a peacock was just the thing.

We were alone on the patio. I decided to take a chance and slipped the mask over his face. It was a wonderful one, carved of brilliantly painted wood. Dad had told us it came from Ceylon, where it was worn by an actor.

"You've never been much of a show-off, Will, but I bet you'd be flirting with Claire if you had half a chance. Never mind; that'll come later. Just for now, strut your stuff. Knock 'em dead, buddy."

God, is this embarrassing. I owe you one for this, Pedro. I'm a peacock all right, but I'm not in the wilds of Ceylon. I'm not in a sultan's private garden. No, I'm in the middle of a damned theme park, right here in the good old US of A. And I'm surrounded by a crowd, all of them pointing cameras at me. What the hell do they want?

I'm pretending not to notice, pecking at popcorn on the grass. Oh, fine. They're following me. I'll just quietly disappear around this henhouse.

Did I say quietly disappear? I am leading a parade of kids. I'm the Pied Piper. I could take these kids anywhere. Bet some of their parents would be grateful, too.

Uh-oh, I've hit a dead end. And now here come the parents, too. I know what they want. They want me to open my tail. Don't they realize I don't perform at the drop of a hat? I need a reason to open my tail, someone I want to impress. Now if Claire were here, I'd put on a show.

Man, this tail is heavy. Think I'd rather be a wren. I'm going to have to fly to the top of this henhouse. Maybe if I perch on top they'll give up. Okay, here goes.

Jeez, what an effort. Not the most elegant of escapes, but it worked. I'm out of their reach now. It's kind of nice up here, too. I can see most of the park. Now I'll scope out a quiet spot, until this whole embarrassing episode is over.

I see just the place. A little yard, cut off by hedges. A few flaps and I'm down. But hold on, I'm not completely alone. There's an old guy here in a wheelchair. Guess he's been left to get a little sun. He's not going to give me any problems, though. Looks like he's dozing off.

Wait, he's not asleep. He's looking at me. Kind of pathetic, him stuck on his own when there's so much going on around him. Wish I could push him around, the way you do me, Pete. Wish I could show him the nuts speeding backward and upside-down on the roller coaster. Or the little kids looking so pleased with themselves, strapped

84

on their wooden horses on the merry-go-round. Maybe I'd get him some cotton candy.

Tell you what, Pete, this is a real bummer, watching this old guy all alone, thinking he was once someone's little boy. And look at him now. But maybe it's all happened before in his life. Maybe he's been on the roller coaster and pigged out on cotton candy. I hope so, Pete. Jeez, I hope so.

His eyes look so tired, like life is a video he's seen too many times. No more surprises for him. He's cocking his bald, bony head. It's as if someone is whispering in his ear.

I think the old guy's dying, Pete. I want to do something. I'm standing at his feet. He's wearing beat-up slippers. There's no one here but me and a dying old man. I can give him something to take with him.

I'm raising the enormous train of my tail. It's heavy. I have to plant my feet firmly and bow slightly to the old man. My tail is high now, arching over me as I spread its bronze feathers. I quiver and the quills of my tail rattle, each feather tipped with a velvety black eye. They're all looking at the old man, daring him to live for just a minute more, before he dies.

Come on, look at this tail! It's dynamite! Look at the colors. And it's all for you. Come on, pal, what do you say?

Hey, maybe he hasn't seen it all, Pete. His thin, dry lips are parting. Hey, Pete, I did it! He's smiling!

I want to get that old one day, Pedro, so old and tired I'm ready to go. No fight. No kicking and screaming.

I know who was whispering in that old man's ear, Pete.

It was Death. He whispered in mine, too. You know what he said, Pete? He said, "Live. I'm coming."

◢◣◢◣◢◣

"Take that thing off his face this instant!"

I reached out to block Kirby's hand as she grabbed the peacock mask. She looked at me, and her eyes were steel-gray lasers.

"What are you trying to do? Smother him?" She pulled the mask off and bent beside Will, holding her fingertips under his jawbone. "I'm barely getting a pulse," she murmured, then glared at me and wheeled him back into the hospital.

I followed, trying to think of how to explain, but I knew that whatever I said would just sound crazy to Kirby, with her sensible shoes planted so firmly on the ground. How could I talk magic to her? It would have been like trying to stop a laser beam with a fairy's wand.

CHAPTER NINE

"MISS MACDONALD!" Kirby's voice cut through the hospital like a knife. I trailed behind her, feeling even more stupid than usual.

Claire came running, out of breath. "What is it, Ms. Kirby?" She looked past Kirby, at me. I rolled my eyes up to the ceiling.

"The patient's breathing is very shallow; his pulse is weak. I want you to help me get him into bed and then monitor his breathing constantly until I get back."

Claire didn't dare ask a question. And Kirby had made it clear that I was to have nothing to do with Will for the moment. He wasn't Will anymore, he was "the patient." Not connected to me.

I stood by helplessly as they got Will back into bed. I stared at Kirby's crisp white back and I hated her. I hated her for thinking I was stupid enough to hurt Will.

She finished tucking him in, took his pulse, and turned on her heel. "Come with me," she ordered. I followed, not knowing what to expect.

She marched to the elevator and just missed one, glancing at her little watch several times. She punched the button twice more and then gave up, pushing through the double doors to the stairs. I followed her up two flights, amazed at how fast she took them.

Breathing hard, we stood for a second outside another unit. The letters ICU were stenciled on the doors in black. I didn't have time to wonder what they were for. Kirby put her finger to her lips and jerked her head in the direction of the doors.

The first thing I noticed was how quiet it was. Not like the kids' unit. No laughter or carts clattering or nurses joking around.

Kirby didn't say a thing as we walked slowly past the beds. None of the patients seemed to notice us. Most of them looked like they just didn't care.

There were people with tubes going into their mouths and noses. That was pretty bad, but some of the tubes even seemed to disappear into holes in their throats. Tubes and wires coming from their chests, from under their sheets. Bags of liquid hanging beside their beds, red, yellow. Stuff was collecting in other bags under their beds. It would have been just plain disgusting if it hadn't been so sad.

Instead of visitors, most of the beds had machines sitting beside them, humming and buzzing. That was the only noise, the humming and buzzing.

The patients mostly had their eyes closed. A few were

staring at nothing. They were all pale. Not like most of the kids in our ward. These people really looked sick.

There was even a kid, maybe a year or two older than Will. There were machines on either side of his bed. I tried to imagine how anyone so young could be that sick. It didn't seem right. I mean, old people sometimes get sick, but young ones, that's different.

I started feeling awful and wanted to get out of there. I shook my head at Kirby. No more. I didn't want to see any more.

She followed me back through the double doors. I could feel her hand on my elbow.

"You'd better sit down," she said. Her hand was still guiding me.

I sat. I was stunned.

"Are you all right?" she asked.

I nodded. "Great," I mumbled.

"It's a frightening place, isn't it, Peter? It's the Intensive Care Unit. It's where patients are taken when they need extra care. Some of them are in danger of dying."

"Will isn't like them."

"Right now, your brother's condition is stable. His breathing is okay."

Of course it is, I thought angrily.

She sat a minute, looking at me, pursing her lips. I stared at the tiny lines above her mouth and wished I could get away from her.

"You mustn't do anything to interfere with that." She waited. "I'm not sure what your mother and father have told you about William's condition."

I didn't answer her. I thought of Mom and Dad, the

way they whispered when I was out of the room. Did I know everything?

All of a sudden my collar felt too tight and there was a burning way back behind my eyes. I was afraid I was going to cry. I looked down at the floor and blinked hard. I could feel her staring at me. I could smell the hospital's smell on her. All starch and medicine and timetables. That was her answer to Will. But it wasn't mine.

"I know Will's going to be all right," I said.

I wanted to sound like I really knew it, like I really knew for a fact that Will was going to be fine, so she could just save her breath and not try to frighten me with a lot of medical mumbo jumbo, because my brother was going to make it. I wanted her to know that, but while I was saying it, it didn't sound like I knew a damned thing. It sounded like I was telling her I knew there was really a Santa Claus.

I wasn't looking at her, but I knew I'd never convince her if I kept staring at the ugly green tiles.

"I think it's important for me to believe that my brother is going to be okay. To know it. Important for Will to believe it, too."

We finally locked eyes, and I was waiting for the put-down look. The look that would say, I'm terribly sorry, dear, but there just isn't a Santa Claus, and your brother is not going to get better.

But instead, it was her turn to stare at the floor. She just sat there for the longest time. Then she said, "You're right, Peter." She said it in a surprised kind of way.

Then she stood up and smoothed the white skirt of her uniform. "I have to go now," she said. It was strange, because it sounded like she was apologizing for ending a really nice time together. "Shall we check on Will?" she asked.

"Yeah," I said, getting up and moving toward the elevator. We waited for it together and I followed her to Will's bed, where Claire was still sitting.

"Any change?" Kirby asked.

Claire chewed her lip for a minute. "I'd say his breathing is slightly better. His pulse is strong." She looked at me as Kirby checked his pulse again. Ever the trusting soul.

The peacock mask was still lying on the bottom of his bed. Kirby picked it up. I held my breath as she examined it. I didn't know what she'd do with it.

"This is lovely, Peter."

"Uh, yeah," I stuttered, surprised by her comment. "It belongs to my dad. He collects them."

"Then he'll want it back, won't he?" She stared at me, just a hint of the old lasers returning.

"Yes," I said, taking the mask from her and wishing the damned thing would disappear.

Kirby left us, and Claire fussed around Will for a while, straightening covers that didn't need it and refilling a full water pitcher. She finally ran out of excuses to hang around and, with her hands on her hips, stood looking at me accusingly. "Are you going to tell me what this is all about?"

"What's what all about?"

She sighed heavily. "The mask. Ms. Kirby. Will's breathing. Where did she take you, anyway?"

I held up my hand. "One thing at a time."

"This is the second time I've seen you with a mask. What's going on, Pete?"

It suddenly all seemed so silly, not like when I talked

to Edgar about it. Claire's frown, her hands on her hips, her whole attitude bugged me. I couldn't tell her. I just couldn't.

Edgar was the one I had to talk to. He knew our secret; he understood what we were doing. He'd know what to do.

"I have to talk to Edgar," I mumbled over my shoulder.

I found him down by the aquarium. He had two little kids with him, one on each hand. All three of them had their noses right up to the tank. Edgar looked like a little kid himself.

"Edgar, can I talk to you when you're finished?"

"Course. Have to get these kiddies back to their mom now, anyway."

The kids started complaining and looked at Edgar like a couple of puppies that wanted to be played with some more. Kids always know a soft touch when they see one.

"I promise to come and get you when it's time to feed the fish again."

The kids smiled.

"And if your mom says you've been very good, I'll even let you pet the fish."

I waited by the tank until Edgar got back.

"Okay, Pete, what's up?" he asked.

"Problems with Kirby."

Edgar's eyebrows shot up. "Come into my office," he said, winking mischievously.

Edgar's so-called office was incredible. A tiny cubbyhole, crammed with junk. It was like he'd bought out an enormous garage sale and stuffed it all into the smallest room he could find. Puzzles, games, records, dolls, puppets, stuffed toys, books, posters, an old football helmet and shoulder pads, a train set, Matilda's cage. And, hanging on a hook, a shabby old Santa costume. It was like I'd been invited to the hiding place of Santa Claus himself.

"Pull up a chair," he said, pointing to a box of books and sitting on one himself. He rested his elbows on his knees and leaned forward. One thing you always knew with Edgar—he was listening to you.

"Kirby caught me with a mask on Will's face and said I was interfering with his breathing and took me around the ICU to scare me."

"Did she ask you what the mask was for?"

I thought. "No, she didn't. She just whipped it off Will's face. She was furious. Then she got Claire to watch Will's breathing while we went up to ICU."

"Then what?"

I shrugged. "Then we just talked. And she seemed to calm down. In fact, she ended up agreeing with me."

"About the mask?" he asked, amazed.

"No, but that it was important for me to know that Will was going to be all right and for him to know that, too."

Edgar smiled his cockeyed smile. "So what's the problem?"

"I'm afraid she won't let me put another mask on him."

Edgar stared at his shoes for a long time. "We're not really sure what the masks are doing, are we? I mean, we're not even sure they're doing anything. When Will had that episode of grabbing your hand, we thought maybe it could have been the poster of that kitten that put the idea into his head, didn't we?"

I nodded. "But what about the turtle mask? How about

when Will turned himself over in bed? And the way the gorilla mask calmed him down. Edgar, I know the masks are doing something. And I know Will wants them."

I was starting to feel desperate. If Edgar lost faith in the masks, I had no ally. And without the masks, what on earth could I do to help Will? Zilch. I could just sit and watch him get worse, like everybody else was doing.

"Edgar, the masks are all I've got."

Edgar was about to say something when the hospital receptionist stuck her head around the door.

"Ah, I thought I saw you two come in here, Edgar. Ms. Kirby's looking for Peter. She thought he might be with you. I'm afraid it's an emergency."

We didn't dare look at each other as we jogged through the halls. My steps, my heart, my brain chanted, Not Will, not Will, not Will.

CHAPTER TEN

"HE'S GONE, Edgar! Christ, even his bed is gone!" I stood in the spot where Will's bed was supposed to be. There was nothing, not even a roll of dust to show that a bed had once been there. A bed with my brother in it.

"Where is he? What have they done to Will?"

"Hold on, Pete. It's okay. I'm sure everything is okay." Edgar had me by the shoulders.

I shook free of him and paced around the room. "Where the hell is Will?" I shouted at Edgar. "What have they done with him?"

"Come on," Edgar said. "We'll find him. I'm sure he's okay, Pete." He started down the hall, and I followed. My heart was racing, telling me to run, but I didn't know which way to go.

Then we saw Kirby. Her face was flushed. "Peter, I've been trying to reach your mom or dad, but there's no answer at home," she said, putting the phone down.

"Will," I shouted. "What about Will? Where is he?"

"He's been put on a respirator, Peter. He stopped breathing. They're monitoring his heartbeat, but he seems to be okay."

"You mean he's in that place? In ICU?"

She nodded and looked at Edgar.

I felt like I was going to be sick, right there, all over those crappy green tiles. "I don't believe you. I have to see him."

"You can't." Kirby's voice stopped me in my tracks. "At least, not yet. Not until Dr. Woodson has examined him and agreed he can have visitors."

"Woodson? What's he going to do? Tap Will's knees and look important? No, thanks. I'll see for myself."

"Not yet, Pete." This time it was Edgar. "ICU's different. You have to play it their way, pal."

I stared down at him and knew he meant it. He had a grip like a vise on my arm.

"Right now, your brother needs rest." Kirby again.

"Rest?" I couldn't believe my ears. "He's been doing nothing but resting in this damned place for the past eight days. And look where that's got him." I turned to Edgar for some support, but he just frowned and shook his head.

"Stop shouting, young man," Kirby ordered, "or I'll ask Edgar to remove you."

I knew I was making a terrible scene, but I couldn't help it. I didn't care who heard me or what they did. I had to see Will, to find out what was really happening to him.

"I'll tell you what Will really needs. He needs to get out of this place. Away from your stupid medical carts and thermometers and charts." I stared at Kirby and Edgar. I was nearly crying and couldn't stop shouting. My hands were shaking and I hooked my thumbs through my belt loops to keep them steady.

"Calm down, Pete. You can't do Will any good like this," Edgar warned.

"In any case, we have to reach your parents."

"Yeah. And what are you going to tell them? That I've stopped Will breathing? That I've put him up there with those people who are waiting to die?"

I saw Kirby give a "help me" look to Edgar.

"Nobody thinks this is your fault, Pete," Edgar said. "We all know you're on Will's side." He loosened his grip on me. "But you've got to remember, we're on his side, too."

I suddenly felt lost. If everybody was on Will's side, why did I still feel so alone? I thought of a dog I once saw running in circles around the bottom of a tree, watching a squirrel that was corkscrewing its way up the tree. The dog didn't see the squirrel hop to the next tree, and just kept running round and round, barking, until his owner dragged him away. That's how I felt, just like that crazy dog.

"Look," I said. I tried to sound calm and cool. "I just want to be able to see my brother. That's all. Just to see him."

"I know that, Peter," Kirby said. "And as soon as Dr. Woodson says it's okay, then we'll take you to ICU."

My mind was racing. Okay, maybe Will was in ICU. So why was Kirby in such a hurry to reach Mom and Dad if he really was okay? Was she telling me everything? Or was there more?

Was Will dying?

"I guess I'll just have to wait," I lied. Waiting was the last thing I was going to do. "I'm not sure where my parents are. Mom was going to have her hair done. But that was this morning, and I don't know where she goes, anyway. And Dad, he might be out getting her a present." I sighed. "Today's her birthday."

The whole time I was talking, I was trying to think of a way to get into ICU.

"You could try Dad's office number. He may have gone to the university." I wrote the number down. "Is it okay if I get a drink?"

"Of course." Kirby sounded relieved. "We'll come and get you when your parents arrive."

"Okay. Edgar, got any spare change? I'll pay you back."

Edgar patted my shoulder and gave me some coins. "This one's on me, Pete."

I nodded and started walking toward the Coke machine in the lobby. How to get into ICU. Just a quick look at Will. Just to make sure he was all right. That's all I wanted.

Now it was my turn to wear a mask, or at least a disguise. I'd never get into ICU looking like myself. I considered all the possibilities. An orderly? I didn't know where to find the clothes. Surely not a doctor. Then I had it. The pajama game.

I waited until the hall was clear and slipped down to Will's old room. Luckily, there was just a janitor, mopping the floor where Will's bed had been.

"Just getting my brother's stuff," I told him. "He's been moved."

He nodded and continued mopping.

I went to his bedside table, where they kept his stuff. Sure enough, they'd forgotten his spare pajamas. I grabbed them and stuffed them into a plastic bag, then went back down the hall.

There were plenty of bathrooms all over the hospital for visitors, and I slipped into one just outside ICU. I went into one of the stalls and put Will's pajamas on, stuffing my clothes into the plastic bag.

I knew there were plenty of people wandering around the hospital in pajamas. No one paid any special attention to them. After all, they belonged there. So all I had to do was wait until the coast was clear, then just walk into ICU and find Will. Easy.

I got to the door and peered through the window. I could see a nurse sitting by the desk where all the monitors are, the ones that show patients' heartbeats. She was bent over some paperwork. Great.

Now came the tricky part. I pushed the doors open very slowly, only far enough to let me slide through. I walked quietly in my bare feet. Once through the door, I slid along the wall slowly, like a slug, checking each room as I passed. Some of the beds were empty. I couldn't see Will yet.

Everything was going fine until a clanking noise started heading my way from the opposite end of the hall. I looked around for a place to hide and ducked into the men's bathroom until the noise was gone.

Back out in the hall, I eased my way toward the desk. Still no Will. Now came the big problem: how to get past the desk so that I could check the other rooms. I knew there were bathrooms at both ends of the hall, but I couldn't just walk by and expect not to be noticed. I needed more of a disguise.

I went into a room with two men. Both of them were sleeping. One of them, the older one, was hooked up to a machine. The other one had dark hair. He wasn't hooked up, and even better, his robe was on the foot of the bed.

I lifted the robe, careful not to disturb him, and slipped it on, turning the collar up high around my neck. I rumpled my hair and picked up the newspaper from the bedside table. I even took his slippers.

Slowly, I began to shuffle toward the bathroom on the other side of the desk. I tried to think about what I'd do if the nurse stopped me, but I just prayed she wouldn't.

Shuffle. Shuffle. Head in the newspaper. A sick man on his way to the bathroom. No need to bother him, Nurse. Just keep moving. Almost past her.

Then it happened.

"Mr. Atkinson? What are you doing out of bed?"

Damn. I stopped dead in my tracks. I could hear the chair squeak as she got out of it. Then her soft, padded footsteps as she came toward me.

I ducked my head further and kept walking, rattling the paper slightly. I'm okay, I thought, just let me past. Shuffle. Shuffle. I wanted to break into a sprint but kept moving along slowly, hoping for a miracle.

Then I got one. I heard this funny noise. *Ping, ping, ping, ping.* I knew that sound. Someone needed help. It was their monitor signaling. The nurse's footsteps stopped. "Wait for me in the bathroom, Mr. Atkinson. I'll be there in a minute."

I made it to the bathroom and went into a stall. I sat on one of the toilets and breathed deeply, trying to calm my heart down. I knew there were only two more rooms. Will had to be in one of them. I stuck my head out of the door. No sign of the nurse, but I knew I didn't have much time. Either Mr. Atkinson would wake up and discover his stuff missing, or she'd come to get me in the bathroom.

I put the slippers into the robe's pocket and snuck across the hall to the next room. He was there. He was alone.

I stood by the bed and looked at him. His eyes were shut. A tube ran from his nose to a machine. I guessed this was the breathing machine. His pajama top was off and there were little discs stuck on his chest. Wires came from these and went to another machine, the heart monitor. Another tube connected his arm to a bag which I knew was feeding him through his vein. Lots of patients had these.

He didn't look as bad as I had expected. They hadn't done anything awful to him. Not yet.

I took his hand. It felt okay. Then I just started talking. I couldn't tell if he heard me. It didn't matter. I was with Will, and he was okay.

"I'm here, Will. I had to sneak in. They think I'm not doing you any good. They want to keep me away. But I'll find a way to get back in. I won't let them separate us. And I won't let them do anything awful to you.

"That tube in your nose is helping you breathe. It looks pretty gross, but I think you need it. Kirby says you stopped breathing. I hope it wasn't the mask, Will. I hope it wasn't my fault."

Will's eyes opened slightly. I leaned way down on the bed so that I'd be in range.

"Anybody home?" I asked.

He stared.

"Hey, Will, I had this amazing dream last night. You know what it was? I dreamed we had a mask adventure together. You didn't do it on your own. I went with you. It was terrific. We were little kids. I can remember pieces of it. Sitting cross-legged in Dad's office. Our knees were touching. I can't remember the details. You know how stupid dreams are, but we were together, Will."

His eyes moved slightly.

I remember, Pete. We were four and six. In the office. With the masks.

"Are you scared, Pete?"

"Yeah."

"Good. Me too. It won't work unless we're scared."

"I want to choose this time, Will. You always get to choose first."

"Okay, okay. Go on, choose."

"I want to be king. The lion."

"Pete, that could be dangerous. It could take you far away. To Africa."

"I still want to be king."

"Okay. Then I'll go with you. I'll be a hyena. Put the mask on. Now hold my hands. Tighter. Stare into my eyes. Ready?"

"Will, I'm really scared. The room is spinning. I feel sick."

"Hold on. It's okay."

"The room is disappearing, going faster and faster."

"Just look at me. Just hold on."

"I can't breathe. I have to scream. Let go, Will!"

"Stop, Pete . . . that noise . . . you're frightening me . . . you're hurting me . . . I'm bleeding . . ."

We can't go together, Pete. It's dangerous. Your dream. It really happened. When we were little. I remember.

"You know I'd do just about anything to be with you. I even thought about falling off my bike and breaking my arm or something so I'd be stuck in the hospital with you. That'd be great, wouldn't it? No one could kick me out then. Not even Kirby.

"What do you say, Will, shall we have another try with the masks? Shall we do it together this time? Do you think we could pull it off?"

Will's eyes seemed to shed their dullness. They flashed. Just for a second, but they flashed.

That's when I knew I had to do it. Somehow I had to get back to Will with another mask.

"I'll be back, buddy. With the masks. We'll take a trip together this time." I pressed his hand and tried to catch his eye. He was staring over my shoulder. But there was something different in his eyes. A warning.

"I think I've heard quite enough." A cold voice sent a chill up my spine. It was the Iceman.

CHAPTER ELEVEN

"I WANT him kept out of this hospital. Is that clear? He's not to be allowed in except when accompanied by his mother or father." Woodson looked down at Edgar, who kept shifting from one foot to the other.

"Is that really necessary? Surely we could—"

"Could what, Ms. Kirby? Could endanger our patient for the sake of an unstable adolescent? I witnessed the bizarre monologue this young man was having with his unconscious brother. A lot of mumbo jumbo about masks and taking a trip together."

Edgar winced and looked down at his shoes.

"I tell you, I'm not having it. I don't know if this is a simple case of sibling rivalry or something more sinister, but it's going to stop. Now. Do I make myself clear?"

Kirby and Edgar nodded, like two little kids.

Woodson wiped his Ben Franklin glasses with a white handkerchief and then folded it neatly, taking his time while we all stood there with nothing to say. Then he walked out of Kirby's office. Icicles hung in the air.

"Well, you heard him, Peter. There's nothing more to be said." Ms. Kirby looked sad but determined.

Tears came burning up from the back of my head. They stung my eyes. I blinked them away, but more kept coming. For once, I didn't care who saw me cry. The whole damned world could watch if they wanted.

Edgar handed me a handkerchief. "Come on, Pete. It's not as bad as all that. Will's going to be okay. You'll be with him again." Edgar wiped his own nose quickly with the back of his hand. "Things just have to settle down. It takes time."

Time, I thought. Somehow I knew time was short. I mopped my face and gave the handkerchief back to Edgar. "Thanks. I guess I'd better change out of these," I said, looking at my pajama disguise. I needed to get away from them, to think.

"If you need to get in touch, I'll be at home," I said to Kirby.

"If there's any change, I'll make sure ICU calls you right away," Kirby said. "Try not to worry too much, Peter. Will's in the safest hands possible."

I tried to force a smile and left to find my clothes. Edgar caught up with me in the hall. "You okay now?" he asked.

"I guess I'm kind of numb." We walked together. I could hear a meal cart rolling our way. "Guess the magic's over."

Edgar blocked my path. He looked angry. "You still don't get it, do you, Pete?"

"Huh?"

"You still believe the masks did it all."

"Well, yeah, I guess I do."

Edgar just kept staring at me, shaking his head. "The magic isn't just in the masks, Pete."

I frowned. "Come on, Edgar. Of course they're magic."

He looked up at me and seemed to square off, like he was going to take a swing at me. "Well, they didn't do much hanging on your dad's wall, did they? Think about it. The magic began when you took them off the wall, when you put them on your brother, when you wanted him to be an animal and move."

I just stood there. I'd never seen Edgar so upset.

"You don't need them, Pete. They're just a prop. All you and Will need is each other. And no one can take that away from you."

He seemed so sure. I wanted to believe him.

"I see magic every time you and Will are together. Like the other day, when you and I took him for a swim in the beast."

I frowned. "What magic? What did you see?"

Edgar shook his head as if he didn't believe me, and sighed. "I'll tell you what I saw. I saw two brothers so close I could hardly tell where one ended and the other began." He pushed his glasses up. "You're standing on a whale, Pete, fishing for minnows." He walked away, still shaking his head slowly.

I changed and rode home in the dusk, thinking about what Edgar had said, about Will, about Mom and Dad and what was going to happen. My brain raced.

I didn't get it. What did he mean, he couldn't tell me from Will? How the hell had he seen any magic when there was none?

I got home and tried to make myself clean up the kitchen

for Mom, but I kept dropping things and forgetting what I was doing. It was no good. I went into Dad's office and sat in his swivel chair, by the phone. I leaned back and propped my sneakers on his desk. The masks were all there.

I tried not to look at them. I kept picking up Dad's anthropology magazines. But in the end, I put them down. The room seemed warm, and I opened the window. I couldn't sit down and began walking back and forth. I could feel myself getting more and more frightened. I tried to fight it, but my fear was growing like a big, ugly weed, right in the pit of my stomach. What did Will call it? The solar plexus. My eyes kept going back to the masks.

I kept thinking about the dream I'd been having. Will and me playing masks when we were little kids. I knew it was important.

I was pacing again. Feeling anxious. Where were Mom and Dad? If only they would call. Or better yet, turn up. Then we could all go to the hospital and see Will together. If I could just talk to someone. Have a normal conversation. Maybe things would stop feeling so strange and scary. I held my hand on the phone, wanting to make it ring. Come on, come on, I kept saying.

Then I heard it. Will's voice. It was as clear as if he was standing next to me, in Dad's office. Only I wasn't hearing it in my ears; it was in my head. "It's okay, Pedro. I'm going." That's all he said, but I knew. I knew right away.

Panic churned my stomach. I wanted to be sick. I picked up the phone, but I knew there was no time. No time to try and find Mom and Dad. No time to speak to Kirby. He was dying. Now. I had to stop him.

"Wait!" I shouted. I looked at the masks. How could I

do it? How could I make them work when Will was so far away? So helpless?

I kept hearing Edgar. "You're standing on a whale, Pete, fishing for minnows." "The magic isn't just in the masks." I could see his lopsided smile as he said it, over and over. "All you and Will need is each other."

All we need is each other. Each other. I flashed on my dream. The lion and the hyena. I could hear the roaring, taste the blood. And then I knew. My roaring! Will's blood! It wasn't just a dream. It had happened. I had attacked him when we were little, playing with the masks. That's why they'd been banned.

Magic was unpredictable, even dangerous. But sometimes it worked. Will and I could make it work. Together.

I was terrified, as if I was on the edge of a cliff and knew I had to jump. If I was lucky, somewhere on the way down, I'd figure out how to fly. I spun around in the swivel chair to face the wall. The masks were waiting.

"Forget the minnows, Edgar. I'm going for the whale!"

I took the fox mask off the wall. I was calm. "I know you can hear me, Will. Listen. We've got to play this game just once more. The way we did when we were little. Together. Just this once. For me, Will.

"You want to go away. That's what you said. Okay, Will. You can go. Escape to the hidden parts of the forest. Go deep in the underbrush. Go as the fox. But look for me. I'll be there."

I stared at the fox's mask. Something dropped onto it as I held it in my shaking hands. A tear? A drop of sweat? My eyes were drawn to the mask's empty eyeholes, and suddenly, as I stared, black became denim blue. The fox's wide eyes held mine. I felt my brother's spirit, like smoke in the room. Then it was gone.

I had to go with him. I had to find him and make him come back with me. But how? I searched the wall for a forest creature. An animal who could sniff out the fox and run with him. There weren't any. I started to panic as my eyes flew over the masks. I had no time. I was losing him.

Who could go into the forest, then? Who could find the fox's scent and track him to his hiding place? My hands reached out in desperation for the only mask that might work.

I held it up to my face and peered through its eyeholes at the fox. I could become this animal and find Will. But then what? What if I attacked him, even killed him, the way the lion had attacked the hyena. Was I making a mistake? The same one I'd made when we were kids, the mistake I relived over and over in my nightmare. But Will was dying. Did I have a choice?

I put the mask on. If Edgar was right, if the magic of the masks came from within me and Will, then maybe we could control it. I had to take that chance. I blinked through the eyeholes at the fox's mask that lay lifeless in my hands.

I would follow my brother, the fox, to his dark, secret places. I would become his mortal enemy, the hound.

▰▰▰▰▰

You got me, Pete. You always do. There I was, slipping quietly away, feeling lighter than a bubble. I was floating. I'd got right to the top of the room, hovering over my bed. But the funny thing was, I could see myself, still lying there. Like being in two places at the same time. But the me in the bed was just a shell, Pete, and I was leaving it behind. I was just going. It wasn't scary. It felt fine. And all I could see was light. I wanted to get to it. I was getting free, Pete.

And then I heard you. Telling me to wait, to play the game again, just this once. Just for you. I came back. Just for you. No one else. Not Kirby or Dr. Woodson. Not the whole freaking hospital could have gotten me back. I did it for you, Pedro. So let's play.

I am the fox. I feel lean and keen and ready for a romp in the woods. I can smell everything. Absolutely everything has a smell—a separate, distinct, unmistakable smell. I'm smelling an acorn that a squirrel has gnawed on. Here's another one. And a squirrel's had a gnaw at it, too. But you know what? It was a different squirrel. My nose is sure of it. Pretty neat, huh?

And I can hear amazing things. Not just squirrels' claws going up trees or blackbirds rustling around in dry leaves. Those are easy. I can hear a wood louse digging its way through the earth. And a tiny wren, far off, scolding a jay for coming too close to its nest. I can even hear a chipmunk scratching a flea.

But suddenly a strange quietness descends, as if a huge bird of prey has spread its dark wings over the woods. A crow is circling high above the tallest pines. Its wing feathers spread against the sky like fingers in black gloves.

Hey, Pedro, we're playing this one together. But who are you? Are you the wren or the chipmunk? Hey, are you the crow?

Far off I catch a glimpse of color. A red that's brighter

than the holly berry, a black darker than night. The colors are frightening, Pete.

I prick up my ears and turn them. There are sounds, not near yet, but coming nearer. There are horns blowing and yelps and bays. They fill the air and they're getting louder. A hunt!

I'm pawing at the ground, feeling nervous. Look for me, you said. But now they're looking for *me*, the hunters and hounds. Where are you, Pete? I thought we were in this one together. Should I go toward the sound? Are you there? Or should I go to earth and burrow for safety? And if I do, will you find me?

I'm moving through the low brush, crouched and silent. The noise is coming nearer, more quickly now. I cross and recross a stream to hide my scent and confuse them.

But I hear a nose sniffing hard at the ground and heavy, clumsy feet crushing the forest floor. I smell hot breath. It's too late to run. I'm scared, Pete. Where the hell are you?

I nose into a nest of brambles. My only chance now is to hide. I'm holding my ears flat on my head as the brambles tear at my coat and cut my paws. I hardly dare to move my ears, to twitch my dry nose.

My God, Pete, one has found me. He's snapping and yelping, snarling. I lie low, spreading my hot body on the cool earth, but it's no good pretending now. This one will have me.

He's crawling, digging, fighting his way through the thick briers. They tear at his face and cut his tongue as he bites them. He slobbers and licks his bleeding lips and nose.

I can hear the other hounds yelping, the horses' hooves pounding. They're closing in. They'll follow this one who's found me. In a minute the pack will be on me. They'll fight over me and tear me to pieces.

Death gleams darkly in the eyes of the hound. He turns them on me, and for the first time my eyes lock with an enemy. An enemy I know.

It's you, Pete. You've forgotten how strong the magic is, how uncontrollable. You've forgotten the lion and the hyena.

We stare at each other through the darkness. Can you fight your instincts? Can you control the magic? I dash from my cover. You're after me. I run, hardly feeling the ground. One last dash for freedom. No hound can be this fast. But you're getting nearer. You're on me, holding me in your teeth, shaking me. I hang limp, waiting. It's okay, Pete. Maybe this was the way it was supposed to happen. Not even a fox can hide from death. But I'm not afraid. You wanted to set me free, Pete. Death will free me now.

You put me down. Gently. I lie on the earth near your paws.

You sit down and throw your head back. I can see blood on your fur. My blood. Your nose points to the dark sky, the circling crow. A howl comes from deep down, from your soul.

I've stopped breathing and stare dully up at you. Are you calling the others in for the kill? A bit of bark falls onto my eye. I cannot feel my heart beating. You sniff me and lightly paw my face.

"Look for me." That's what you said, Pete. I blink, and the bark slides, clearing my vision. You stand over me, your head cocked. I look into my enemy's eyes and find you, Pete, mastering the magic, willing me to live. I gasp for air. My heart is pounding in my chest!

We're leaping, yelping, running together. The fox and the hound. We leave the others far behind. The forest is ours, Pedro. The whole freaking world is ours!

We're riding the whale, buddy. Wish Edgar could see us.

CHAPTER TWELVE

"PETER! My God, are you all right?"

"Can you get up, Pete?"

That was the next thing I remember. Mom and Dad helping me up off the floor of Dad's office.

"You're so pale, Peter. Did you faint?" Mom asked.

I shook my head and sat in Dad's chair, trying to remember what had happened. I looked at the floor. The fox and hound masks were lying there. Then it all came back.

"Will's okay!" I nearly shouted.

"Of course he is. We're going to see him now."

"No. I mean he wasn't okay. They moved him to intensive care. And he died. But he's back now." The words came bubbling up in my throat. "I made him come back."

Mom and Dad kept asking questions in the car, all the way to the hospital. I knew they were worried, and I wanted to make them know I wasn't crazy, but I was so excited, I couldn't stop jabbering about the Iceman and the masks and how I heard Will call to me. And how I knew he was dying.

They listened and tried to make sense of it. Dad was really upset.

"I should have realized you were using the masks. I kept feeling something was wrong when I was in my office, but I could never put a finger on what it was." Dad slammed his open palm on the steering wheel. "Damn."

But the great thing was, I could tell why Dad was upset. It was because he believed me. He believed every word of it.

His hands were shaking as he ground the car into gear. "I knew I should have gotten rid of those masks years ago, when you boys first started to play with them."

"But don't you see, Dad? The masks helped."

Our eyes met in the rearview mirror. For a second it was just like looking at Will. He didn't say anything.

We got to the hospital and went straight up to ICU. There was a group gathered just outside the doors: Ms. Kirby, Dr. Woodson, Edgar, Claire, and the nurse who'd been on duty in ICU when I went in. They were all there, talking in whispers. But they shut up when they saw us.

"Is he all right?" Dad almost shouted. "Is my son all right?" He nearly grabbed Dr. Woodson by the lapels.

And for once, the Iceman didn't seem so cool. "Something quite extraordinary has occurred," he said. "I'm not exactly sure what to make of it."

Edgar was standing next to a respirator that he'd just pushed through the ward doors. He looked pale and talked to me in a whisper. "He's okay," he said, squeezing my shoulder. "Will is fine. Now."

Even Kirby seemed kind of dazed. She was sitting on the

sofa beside Claire and had hold of Claire's arm. "I've never known anything like it," she said to no one in particular.

"It seems that while this young lady was on duty in ICU, your son's heart stopped beating." Iceman looked at the nurse, who nodded her head. Mom and Dad looked at me.

"It happened so suddenly," the nurse explained. "By the time we were ready to try and revive him, he was alive." She said this as if she didn't even believe it herself. "His heart had started beating again."

Dr. Woodson was polishing his glasses, but his hands were shaking. "I've read of cases of, shall we say, a spontaneous return to life, but some time had passed between your son's apparent death and subsequent revival." He was rubbing his glasses so hard that I thought the friction might melt them. "And the strange double twist to all this is that William's vital signs—that is, his pulse, his heart, but mainly his breathing—have quite suddenly taken a turn for the better." Dr. Woodson seemed mystified. The guy was human. "In fact, I've taken him off the respirator. He'll stay on the heart monitor for now." He looked at the floor and shook his head. "Extraordinary," he said to himself. "Quite extraordinary. Your son is a very lucky young man."

I grinned. Maybe you could call it luck.

"Can we see Will now?" Mom asked.

"Yes," Dr. Woodson said. "But please go in very quietly and stay for only a few minutes."

"Of course," Dad said, taking Mom by the arm.

When we got to his bed, Will was asleep. He'd been disconnected from the respirator, just like Dr. Woodson said.

Mom sat by his bed just looking at him for the longest time. Dad stood behind her, resting his hands on her shoulders.

I was dying to talk to Will, but I wanted Mom and Dad to have their time with him.

Mom picked up one of his hands and held it to her lips. Will's eyes opened slowly and lazily. They roamed around the room as if they were looking for something. Finally they settled on Mom.

Will looked different. His color was better. But there was something else, something different.

Then he looked at me and I knew. His eyes were open. Almost all the way. Wide enough for me to see a spark in them.

Mom kissed him and so did Dad. Dr. Woodson signaled us it was time to leave. Claire, Kirby, and Edgar were standing in the background, trying to get a peek at Will. Like a little cheering section.

"We'll keep him in ICU for another day," Dr. Woodson explained when we were back outside the unit. "Just to be sure. And he'll be in the hospital for some time. But as far as I can tell, your son has started to improve. Normally this takes much more time, anywhere from days to weeks or even months. The typical case, if there is such a thing, is of the patient getting gradually weaker, then leveling off—reaching a plateau, as we say. Then, finally, improving."

"Will seems to have speeded the process up," Dad said. I could see how relieved he was. He seemed like his old self again for the first time since the whole nightmare began.

"So it appears," Dr. Woodson agreed. And then this incredible thing happened. A tiny crack between Dr. Woodson's thin lips. A glimpse of tooth. A whole bunch of teeth. The Iceman smiled! I could hear the melting icicles dripping all around us.

This seemed to be Kirby's cue. "So Will may be back on my floor in a day's time?"

I loved it: "My floor."

Dr. Woodson nodded.

Claire giggled. "I can't wait to tell Millie!"

Kirby frowned at Claire.

Edgar winked at Kirby.

Finally she remembered who and where she was. She examined her little upside-down watch and walked briskly to the elevator. "Miss MacDonald, it's time to return to the floor." Claire followed obediently, and as the doors of the elevator closed, we could hear Kirby's voice. "There are bedpans to be emptied, water pitchers to be filled . . ."

"I must be going as well," Dr. Woodson said. "I'll check William first thing in the morning."

"Thanks," Dad said as he put his arm around Mom's shoulder. "Happy birthday," he said, and kissed her on the cheek. They walked with Dr. Woodson to the elevator.

"I'll take the stairs," I called as Edgar and I walked together. We ended up, as usual, at the aquarium.

Edgar raised the lid and tapped on the surface of the water. Seraphim came straight up, and Edgar petted him. Then he sprinkled some food in, and all the fish took their places, the bottom feeders safely waiting for the food to trickle down to them. Seraphim and a few others went right up to the surface.

"Top feeders," I said.

Edgar winked. "Takes one to know one." He put the lid down and stowed the fish food behind the aquarium. "Pete, I was watching you," Edgar said. "You didn't seem at all surprised when Dr. Woodson said Will's heart had stopped and started again."

"I wasn't," I said. "I was with him the whole time."

Edgar whistled softly and pushed his glasses back up.

"Come on, Peter," Mom called as she and Dad stepped off the elevator. "Time to go home."

"See you tomorrow, Pete?" Edgar asked.

"Sure thing. Have to get started on Will's physical therapy now that he's on his way back."

Edgar looked excited. "Say, I came across a great book, all about rebuilding muscles and learning to walk again. Walking might be difficult for Will at first." Edgar was sort of running alongside me, trying to keep up as I followed Mom and Dad. "Hold on a minute. I want to read something to you." And he dashed back to his office.

I shouted to Mom and Dad that I'd be out in a second.

Edgar came back, out of breath. He had this enormous book that someone had donated to the hospital. "Listen to this, Pete." He pushed his glasses back and read, " 'To walk we have to lean forward, lose our balance, and begin to fall.' " He stopped and looked up at me. "That's what it's all about, isn't it? Having the courage to lose our balance. Pretty good, eh?"

I laughed. Edgar and his books. But then I tested it out on the way to the car. I walked really slowly. And like Edgar said, for each step, I had to lean forward, lose my balance for a moment, begin to fall, and then catch myself with the other leg.

Will could do that. And even if he fell a couple of times, that'd be all right. I'd be there. I'd catch him.

AFTERWORD

The rare illness that paralyzed Will Chisholm is called Guillain-Barré syndrome. It can occur at any age and in both sexes. It affects the peripheral nerves of the body and can cause weakness, paralysis, and abnormal sensations. Guillain-Barré syndrome can vary tremendously in severity from a mild case to a devastating illness with almost complete paralysis, bringing a patient close to death.

Help and information for sufferers and their families exists through contact with the Guillain-Barré Syndrome Foundation International, National Office, P. O. Box 262, Wynnewood, PA 19096.